TWELVE MONTHS OF FREEDOM

———•⚛•———

PETER KENNEDY

Copyright © Peter Kennedy 2019
This book is sold subject to the condition that it shall not, by way of trade or otherwise, be lent, resold, hired out, or otherwise circulated without the publisher's prior consent in any form of binding or cover other than that in which it is published and without a similar condition including this condition being imposed on the subsequent publisher.
The moral right of Peter Kennedy has been asserted.
ISBN-13: 9781086043976

For Catherine

This is a work of fiction. Names, characters, businesses, places, events and incidents are either the products of the author's imagination or used in a fictitious manner. Any resemblance to actual persons, living or dead, or actual events is purely coincidental.

CONTENTS

CHAPTER 1 *The Irrational Plan* 1
CHAPTER 2 *January - A visual feast* 9
CHAPTER 3 *February - A myriad of sounds* 23
CHAPTER 4 *March - A gastronomic experience* 35
CHAPTER 5 *April - A touch of class* 45
CHAPTER 6 *May - The sweet smell of failure* 52
CHAPTER 7 *June - The grandeur all around us* 61
CHAPTER 8 *July - The magnificent structures humans build* 72
CHAPTER 9 *August - Food for thought* 82
CHAPTER 10 *September - The realm of literary possibilities* 92
CHAPTER 11 *October - A good time to be unselfish* 100
CHAPTER 12 *November - The reality behind the screen* 110
CHAPTER 13 *December - The cycle of life and death* 117

CHAPTER 1

The Irrational Plan

When engrossed in a demanding profession there is the world of work and also brief, but necessary, periods of not working. The external world is largely irrelevant to the truly committed. But when you have retired or resigned from a lifetime's position for all kinds of possible reasons, and therefore no longer working, everything suddenly changes. Then there is only the world as it really is and yourself. Or at least that's how it seemed to Judge Richard McQuade. You can then choose to be either in the world or not in the world. While some people may just retreat into and gain some comfort from their own private sanctum of consciousness, a few others – perhaps the brave ones – who no longer want to live in the present reality, decide to exit this world by taking their own lives. In modern parlance that's a form of 'taking control.' While that course may seem at first glance to be perverse – even insane to be frank – it does have a certain logic to it, or at least that's how it seemed to him about a year ago. That's when he decided, entirely on his own accord, to quit his high-powered legal position in favour of what he had erroneously thought would be a better quality of life, or at least a life that promised some relief from the huge stress of being a well-respected and hard-working Circuit Court Judge.

How wrong can you be?

He made his decision to quit in the late summer of 2017 and settled on a leaving date of Christmas, just four months later. But it was during the month of October, while still working diligently at his busy and highly responsible job of pontificating while at the same time making difficult, if not nearly impossible, judgements affecting peoples' lives, that the real seeds of doubt about his decision began to take hold in earnest.

He had a feeling of despair, a total lack of self-worth, largely because he was truly defined by his everyday work (like so many people are, or at least say they are), and, despite his unusually wide interests outside the Law, and having what many others thought, rightly or wrongly, to be an unusually fine intellect, he felt his life was effectively over. And, in a sense, of course it was. While many hard-working professionals embrace retirement with an enthusiasm that is remarkable in both its intensity and sheer enjoyment of life's everyday pleasures, such as a greater involvement with family, getting up late and the strange allure of the golf course, that was certainly not the case for him. In short, he hated not working and the empty feeling that such a state induced in him. If he is to be truthful, he also greatly missed the undoubted respect that he induced in his colleagues and the general public in virtue of both the elevated position in the law and his countless fair and wise judgements.

There is no question about this: His Honour Judge Richard McQuade QC, OBE, was a well-respected and almost certainly popular Circuit Judge based in London. Well, that is what he chose to think about how he was perceived, at least in retrospect. For the benefit of those who may possibly be unfamiliar with the subtleties of British law, the initials 'QC' stand for Queen's Counsel, which is a title given only to the most eminent members of our legal profession, be they barristers (in most cases), lawyers and judges (though usually the latter have generally been barristers for many years). But you don't, of course, have to be a QC to be a judge. It just so happens that he was, but he never reached the highest echelons of the profession, which is to become a High Court Judge, but he will ruminate about that later.

Perversely, but in his personal worldview, quite logically, he decided that suicide was a definite option though if he carried it through to its conclusion then it would need to be as painless and non-traumatic as possible, if that is not a contradiction in terms. But before he could summon up the required courage and enthusiasm for such an irreversible and drastic course of action, he needed to be sure that it was justified, assuming such an act can *ever* be justified. Now there's an interesting medico-legal issue. Or maybe it's just an ethical issue. And also, one mustn't forget the devastating effect that violent act of self-extinction would have on his understanding wife and three adult children. Maybe that would be the most selfish and stupid thing that he could ever do. But if so, then he would just have to add it to all the other stupid mistakes he'd made during his (mostly pretty miserable) sixty-seven years on this lonely planet of ours.

So, he formulated a plan to decide whether or not he would kill himself, and a particularly irrational one it was for sure now he thinks about it in retrospect. He thinks it's best to be honest and direct about this sad business and call a spade a spade. He would imbibe and indeed expose himself to every key emotional and physical stimulus that he could think of, ideally one theme for every month of the year, to see whether any of these experiences would induce him to change his mind about whether life is really worth living, with the inevitable result that he would no longer consider prematurely terminating his own life. While that plan seemed eminently logical at the time, he realises, of course, that most people would not agree with him, citing perhaps a temporary imbalance of the mind, probably a reactive depression due to not working, combined with its associated lack of self-esteem, a state of affairs that would reverse itself in due course, either with or without medication. There was no way he was going to take any drugs for what was clearly an unusual view of the world, rather than a symptom of some psychiatric illness. It really was not an illness; he can assure you. He was, and indeed still is, a completely rational being. He knows he is not a medical doctor, and certainly not a psychiatric one, but he also knows for certain that he is not mad. Why would anyone think otherwise? Anyway, it's all of little importance in the grand scheme of things, and by the time you read this (or I should say *if* you read this) he will have long departed.

Where that will be to, we don't yet know. Nor can you know, unless you're God of course, which obviously you can't be (as far as we know).

So, to get back to the task in hand, he had to identify a total of twelve potentially life-enhancing experiences to see whether any of them could make him sufficiently positive to dissuade him from his intended course of action after one year. That is not as straightforward as you might think. Five, naturally, were easy being the classical five senses, namely those of sight, hearing, taste, touch and smell. He could think of many ways in which life can present these to us in a multitude of guises. But what about the other seven? We have so far only reached June, assuming he starts his experiment in January. So, he thought harder and came up with what ended up as being additional and entirely bespoke sensory experiences, those he had engineered just for this purpose and which had real meaning for him. Can one call that personalised medicine? It's more like precision death.

So, here's what he came up with for all twelve sensory or spiritual experiences which would take him right up to the month of December, traditionally a month suffused with joy and celebration. Well, not everything in life (or death) fits in neatly with tradition.

During January he would immerse himself in paintings and visual beauty as depicted in art galleries and museums. For February he would experience the world of musical sound, both in concert halls and through earphones. March would suffuse him with the pleasures of food, both in restaurants and at home. During April he would try hard to rejuvenate his interest in the world of feeling and touch if that were somehow possible. Now, that would take some thought and innovation. May could pose a problem but journeys to sweet-smelling flower gardens both in his city and beyond might suffice. June will be a kind of continuation of May and will be spent admiring the natural beauty all around us and for this he is ideally placed, living in a country replete with a host of picturesque areas of great tranquillity and demureness. In July he would spend the month visiting and trying to appreciate great buildings and feats of engineering in the hope that architectural and structural beauty will move him just enough to make a difference. August would find him engrossed in intellectual pleasure as he immerses himself in the works of some of the great philosophers and thinkers, including those with whom he is most familiar and greatly admires. In a similar vein he would spend September reading the novels of some of his favourite writers- but here only the best will do. Just in case you think he is completely self-obsessed (which actually he is but let's not worry about that now) he will devote October to voluntary work, helping others, including those who are unable either through illness or advanced age to do things for themselves. Now that's bound to make him feel better about life and perhaps even himself.

November will be another entirely selfish month in which he will watch as many films as possible in many different genres and time periods in the hope that such escapism may somehow release him from his current mindset. Then, finally, he will contemplate and, he hopes, appreciate the majesty and vastness of the Universe during December when he will spend every evening gazing at the night sky when the wispy cloud cover allows him to. He will also contemplate the existence of God. Then around Christmas he will make a final decision and will or will not act before the New Year. Well that doesn't sound too difficult does it?

CHAPTER 2

January - A visual feast

The ability to see everything around us, one that firmly anchors our consciousness in what we perceive as the real and only world, is perhaps the most valuable of all our sensory gifts. Yet like all gifts, we have a terrible tendency to take this facility for granted. But there is a definite difference between looking and seeing, don't you think? While everyone is capable of looking, it takes a particular effort to see and perceive the intrinsic beauty of our surroundings. A developing human child, so his neurological acquaintances tell him, has to learn to see the world as its nervous system matures, but he suspects some of us never truly see very much of the world as it really is even though we may be fully mature, at least in the physical sense if not the emotional one. But here he is being too judgemental which is a tendency that he must forget and leave behind forever. For that attitude was part of a very different life, a time and a worldview that has now passed, one that furnishes many memories, some good and others not so good. And if there is one thing he just refuses to be, it is a human anachronism.

So, he had to decide where to start in his exploration of visual pleasure and inspiration. The obvious place to start would be in an Art Gallery, and for certain the great city of London has plenty of those. As a Judge working primarily in the London Circuit, he has lived in England's capital city for his entire life, apart from a one-year sabbatical period in Philadelphia when he was a trainee lawyer and that was so long in the past that it almost eludes any clear notion of personal history. His memory is good but not that good, and besides, it wasn't altogether a particularly happy time so there may be an element of selective amnesia there. That's just the kind of rather convenient memory lapse that he has seen so often in the witnesses who have testified before him in the Courts. That is hardly surprising for a Judge concerned almost entirely with criminal cases as he was for nearly fifteen years. But whenever he could, he always used to give people the benefit of the doubt. Whether that is a strength or a weakness in making judgements he will never know for sure. He thinks that's up to others to decide.

Maybe they already have. Wherever you live in the Northern Hemisphere, January is generally a pretty miserable month in terms of weather. He always associates it with snow, penetrating cold and icy pavements on which you can slip easily, and to be quite honest about it, he regards it as the worst month of the year. He is not surprised that so many elderly people die during January. All those broken hips that his medical friends have to replace at this time testify to the intrinsic danger of this month. And after all, both his parents died of double pneumonia during January, though that was ten and fifteen years ago, leaving just fragments of memories which, through the strange portal of time, seem to coalesce into just pleasant recollections though he has no doubt there were also plenty of darker moments on both sides lurking behind the happy facade. But they are visual memories and not true visions, and for these he needed to be stimulated into action or else inaction by the sight of pictorial beauty, strong colours and striking visual imagery.

Travel by public transport within London is so efficient and extensive (though increasingly expensive, even for him on a Judge's generous and gold-plated pension) that he encountered no difficulty in travelling on the London underground and buses to the galleries and museums of his choice. He considers that he's not a very original person, and that's probably just as well given his profession which requires a cool and logical head, though he knows he's thoroughly sensible and broad-minded, at least when he's dealing with other people and not himself. So, somewhat predictably, he honed-in on places he knew by reputation but had not visited himself since he was a young man. He therefore chose The National Gallery in Trafalgar Square, The National Portrait Gallery sited just next to it, The Tate Galleries (both Tate Britain in Westminster and Tate Modern in Bankside), and The British Museum in Bloomsbury. Pretty conventional Institutions for sure but he is always attracted to quality which all these places certainly possess. Anyway, what's wrong with being conventional? You have probably guessed by now that he also does not practice political correctness. That's another, perhaps more cogent, reason for departing this world. But he really mustn't be so cynical (though that's a difficult one for him). Actually, he has no need to operate in such a ridiculous 'PC' way since he regards fairness and broad mindedness as a *sine qua non* of his erstwhile position. Universal politeness and an unwavering and intrinsic respect for one's fellow human beings would necessarily banish political correctness to the realm of history.

But, unfortunately, many people, and perhaps most, just aren't like that. He knows that for sure and can speak with considerable authority from over forty years' experience dealing with all sorts of folk. Hence the modern insanity that pervades our culture and constantly keeps us on our toes as if we are forced to walk on glass shards, ever mindful of the pitfalls into which we might so easily plunge. But what can you do? Nothing at all.

It took him about forty-five minutes to make his way from his comfortable, detached four-bedroom house in North London to Leicester Square station in central London from where he walked the short distance along the strangely claustrophobic but familiar main road to the magisterial National Gallery. As he ascended the steep steps from the right side, he looked back instinctively to the tall and iconic Nelson's Column, an edifice to one of the nation's enduring military heroes and a man for whom he had always felt an odd combination of admiration and compassion. He never quite understood why so many people admired this great figure without a keen awareness of the sheer tragedy of his cruelly curtailed life and his many medical conditions that he tolerated with such fortitude. He also wondered whether the poor man was cold and lonely up there, being placed on a pinnacle so high and subjected on a daily basis to the impersonal humiliation of a multitude of disrespectful pigeons. Why does he always see the human side of what is merely a statue, an historical reminder of what has gone before? Please don't ask or even try to answer that question.

He entered the imposing classical building and walked briskly and purposefully into its stylish foyer. Immediately he had an instinctive feeling as to which artists and paintings would have the greatest impact and might just help him to see everything in his life with more clarity. Some of these he had probably seen before, either in their original form or in the visual media, while others he had only imagined he had seen, possibly in his dreams. Perhaps in some cases both were true. To be frank, he neither knew for certain nor truly cared. He has always been unable to spend more than about ninety minutes gazing at pictures in a Gallery because he becomes saturated with visual imagery very quickly and his head literally starts to spin, and that isn't helped by the indefinable but curious odour that emanates from Institutions like these. That is why he always needs to be selective in what he looks at. Aren't most people the same? Actually, from his own experience, in many respects, almost all people are the same. Please note the word 'almost.'

Here he must admit to a fundamental problem he has with looking at any painting, though this hardly applies to photographs. Why is he affected more by some paintings than others? He thinks a particular image sets off something that is already inside his head rather than it being merely the only cause of a human emotional reaction. He is looking for a type of experience that enables him to realise, or actually recapture, something that is already there. The picture reactivates or rescues inner visions which have probably lain dormant for years within a person's consciousness and somehow brings them to the surface and, of course, the intrinsic impact and originality of the painting itself sparks off new reactions which can then interact with and reinforce the original feelings which it caused to emerge in the first place. But this is far too self-centred, and he is, as an old school teacher once suggested to him, becoming confused by the labour of his own thinking. The reality of the situation is that some paintings are intrinsically so magnificent in their technique and imagery that they introduce the viewer to visions that had never been perceived before. Now there's a thought, and anyway, how does any of this help to resolve his deathly problem? It doesn't. But that doesn't stop them being wonderful paintings.

He has always been entranced by landscape paintings, far more than portraits which more often than not scare the living daylights out of him, though he has no idea why that should be so. Maybe it is a remnant of his childhood fear of puppets, especially when they were grotesque caricatures of living or imaginary human creatures. He was terrified, not spellbound or amused, by Punch and Judy with their thin veneer of violence, and even more upset by some of the frightening caricatures of imagined nobility he watched on television. That was what might now be called a bad learning experience. As he strolled through the never-ending and interconnected chambers of the famous Gallery, he calmly imbibed the numerous pastoral images before him, some striking and others rather less so. While he was wildly appreciative of the exquisite portrayals of famous and idealised rural landscapes encapsulated by John Constable in captivating works such as 'The Hay Wain' and 'The Cornfield', nevertheless their beauty, often sporting a tiny dot of red in their centre, did not change his mood or even come near to it. That surprised him as he had been expecting the opposite. But then he found himself in a rather intimate room containing the works of the old Dutch masters. He was as struck as ever by the genius of Rembrandt, so obvious in the large collection on display, but his early self-portrait, in which he looks considerably older than his years, did not frighten Richard in the least and succeeded in what may well have been one of his aims in that it filled him with a sense of compassion. Mind you, having said that, he has always been easily moved to compassion by relatively mundane human events so that was no surprise, at least to him. Surely that is a good character trait for a Judge? He thinks it must be, so long as it is tempered with a sense of proportion and justice. It would be so good to have a definitive answer to that one, though perhaps it might function more effectively as a demanding examination question for a University legal degree. A sense of cultivated pomposity knows no limits.

Soon after that he came across a series of paintings that moved him in precisely the way in which he had hoped. Perhaps they recreated a series of previous memories, or maybe it was an entirely novel phenomenon. The artist who accomplished this was the Dutch painter Meindert Hobbema, a man who died when he was only four years older than Richard was at the time. In those early eighteenth-century days, however, seventy-one years old wasn't a bad innings at all. Nowadays he thinks we would regard such a lifespan as tantamount to being short-changed. Please remember he thought that. It's significant.

What was it about this artist's work that affected him so greatly? He will probably never know for certain, but perhaps it was his unusual ability to make him want to live in the villages, among the country folk and be part of the rural idylls that he managed to portray in such a direct manner. There was also what can best be described as a muscular physicality and richness of the artist's brushstrokes that managed to reach right through to his imagination. Richard truly wanted to be in those places. While naturally he also appreciated the broad Dutch landscapes depicted by his teacher Jacob van Ruisdael, he still preferred the visual imagery of his apprentice. In some mysterious way the thick circular vividness and rustic colours of

Hobbema's brushwork somehow penetrated the contours of his imagination, and this resulted in what can only be described as a delicious combination of tranquillity and pleasure. He wondered what the artist would have thought had he heard him say this. It does sound a bit over the top and flowery. He guessed he would have been quite pleased but also would have also thought him somewhat mad. Perhaps he is, just a little. He doesn't know yet.

That first time he visited the National Gallery to find pictures that would resonate with, and maybe even assuage, his morbid state of mind, he grew weary within an hour. But not before he had found what had been, until then, one of his favourite British paintings, the sublime and enigmatic mythical portrayal of Dido building Carthage by none other than Joseph Mallord William Turner, arguably the greatest painter in our island's history. How he loves this painting, with its exquisite contrasts of bright sunlight and gloomy buildings, Arcadian imagery, tall vegetation and shimmering river, not to mention the implications of a tragic future for its main character. He thought he knew something of what she felt, though naturally for entirely different reasons. This picture had the overall effect of appealing to his imagination and feelings of compassion, without assaulting his personality, in the nicest possible sense of the word. He was glad to have seen it again in the flesh, so to speak, but it still affected his psyche less than some of the other landscapes, at least at that difficult time.

That was enough for him at the beginning of January, a few days after the widespread but routine celebrations of the New Year. He visited the magisterial Gallery three more times that month, usually staring at the same paintings but also, as you would imagine, his gaze took in the works of many other artists across several centuries and from many European studios. But he never again experienced the emotional impact of that first pictorial adventure. During that month he also explored the three other Institutions, with two separate visits in each case. He was keen to see the large collection of Turners at the Tate Britain and, while he admired their sheer panache and originality, none moved him as much as the image of Dido had done earlier during his search. As for the Tate Modern, here he must admit to what he supposes is a failing in his aesthetic appreciation as he seldom sees great virtue in the purely modern art form. He admired the sheer cleverness and imagination that was so evident in many paintings and sculptures, but none moved him or assaulted his personality as much as he had either hoped or expected. He has always had a soft spot for, and an appreciation of, Henry Moore's sculptures but that might well be a partial consequence of an admiration of the man himself. One thing that he kept asking himself is how many of the modern artists, particularly those who paint in the abstract form, also have the capability of drawing and painting in the more classical style. He always imagined they would have had to demonstrate such ability to gain entry to Art School in the first place, so he had deduced that the answer to his silent question is presumably most, if not all, of them. But yet he has a sneaking suspicion that he may not be absolutely correct about that. While some modern artists are no doubt brilliant in many styles, but just choose to paint in a very modern, and sometimes abstract way, others may have somehow escaped that route. But who is he to judge in such matters? He is not an expert.

He was somewhat mesmerised at the comparatively new white structure and masterly layout of ancient and more modern exhibits at The British Museum, not that far from his old legal haunt, and at one point thought he might be as deeply affected by all that he saw as he had been when confronting Hobbema and Turner. But on his second visit there he was less convinced about that. The Museum is a gem and a masterpiece for sure and he derived a good deal of pleasure from strolling through its elegant pathways, including those on an elevated plane, but when he finally left, though he had been aesthetically poleaxed by its historical virtuosity and brilliantly constructed design, he had not actually been emotionally transfixed to the extent that he had sought.

But all things considered, he had made a promising start. He had staved off suicide for at least a month because of the perception of artistic genius and kindred spirits and was convinced that he was definitely a person who could be ultimately rescued.

CHAPTER 3

February - A myriad of sounds

He just can't imagine what it must be like to be completely deaf. He continues to marvel at many deaf peoples' remarkable ability to master sign language and lip read with such amazing facility. Occasionally, he has had to deal with such people, in different contexts of course, in his Court cases when it is vital to employ the sympathetic talents of a sign language interpreter, and that seems to work fairly well. But there must be a huge chasm between losing one's hearing and never being able to hear in the first place. The same kind of issue can also be applied to vision, of course, when there must be an enormous emotional difference between losing this vital ability and never having had the gift of sight from birth. He personally imagines that the first of these tragic scenarios would be far worse, but who is he to make such a lordly judgement? In any case, both types of sufferers have, out of necessity, to master the intricacies of Braille, assuming they still have the sense of touch, and frankly he doesn't think he would have the emotional capacity or even stamina to deal with any of these terrifying situations. He may judge and think he feels for others, but, in reality, no-one can really do that from the outside. A person blind from birth can never truly see red, and someone who has always been deaf will never be able to appreciate Mozart. Even Beethoven could hear everything normally before he went deaf.

What millions of years of evolution have achieved in allowing humans and animals to see and hear has always amazed Richard. If we consider hearing, most of what he knows has been gleaned from listening to his medical and scientific counterparts, occasionally in giving expert testimony in medical negligence cases, as well as the little he has understood from popular medicine books which are essential reading for him, though in confidence he doesn't always understand everything he reads. Does anyone? Just think of it.

Sound waves pass through air and enter one's body through the outer ear, the different shapes of which have always had the capacity to amuse him for some strange reason. That is not meant to be rude. He is noted for his courtesy and polite demeanour which is entirely appropriate and consistent with his high judicial status, or, more accurately, his erstwhile high status. Then the sound waves hit the three little bones called ossicles in the middle ear which transmit the vibrations to the fluid-filled cochlea in the inner ear which contains specialised hair cells which then convert the vibrations into nerve impulses. These impulses travel along a nerve called the eighth or auditory nerve which reaches the cerebral cortex of the brain. The part, he gathers, that receives and processes these impulses in the superior (upper) part of the temporal lobe of the cerebral cortex. Now that's not bad for a simple layman is it? Sometimes he even surprises himself. But that part of the brain must, he presumes, be connected to, or at least converse with, other parts that are concerned with memory, pleasure and such things. The reason he thinks this is because some sounds and also voices just irritate the hell out of him, though anyone observing him would never know. He is very good at concealing his personal opinions and emotions. He is not that upset at the classical disagreeable sounds such as chalk scratching annoyingly on a blackboard or the high-pitched screeching of a car's brakes. No, what really gets to Richard is a very soft clipped manner of speech, you know the type, the person with so-called perfect diction with all the t's and d's articulated very correctly and precisely. He just can't stand people speaking with such clipped consonants, but he is not upset by upper class 'posh' speech *per se*. After all, he speaks pretty well himself, having attended a private school (because of his brains and not his parents' bank balance) and with a good Oxford degree. But he still doesn't speak like that in all its affectations. He knows some clever neuroscientists have identified the parts of the visual cortex at the back of the brain which are important in giving us the sense of visual discomfort. So, his question is whether there is also a part of the brain that is concerned with aural discomfort, not from very loud noises, but from sounds that emanate from such highly annoying people. If there are, then are they the same areas that control our responses to other irritating noises such as not-so-loud screeches? He thinks these are good questions that scientific ignoramuses like him are more likely to ask than the so-called experts. Sound can be a true delight or else a gigantic pain in the arse.

So let's return to his problem, aim, search, or whatever you want to call it (assuming you want to call such an absurd activity anything at all). His aim in February was to acquire stimulation for life from the sheer pleasure of sound. He never thought even a superficial knowledge of the aural mechanism would detract in the slightest degree from the power that the right set of sounds would exert on his already fragile state of mind. And so it turned out.

But where was he to start? The answer may be obvious to anyone with a passionate appreciation of the mathematical and exquisite harmony and subtle modulations that characterise so much of the music of Johann Sebastian Bach. Or perhaps it's not obvious to anyone at all. Anyway, there's a musical genius for sure. Mozart was also a genius of course and a remarkable child prodigy to boot, but he knew in his heart that he had to start off with the sublime music of JS Bach. Now there's a surprise to be sure. But he makes no arrogant judgements whatsoever in this regard – *Chacun à son goût* as they say. So, he spent the first three days of the month listening to nothing but Bach's choral and keyboard works through his so-called noise-less high-end earphones which transmitted many of his finest compositions from his iPod to the music centres of his brain, wherever they are. This process of musical appreciation leading to the highest level of spiritual enlightenment and pleasure remains a complete mystery to him. He did once see a young man in his Court who developed major seizures whenever he was elevated to auditory ecstasy by the fourth and final movement of Beethoven's ninth symphony but that's another story, and frankly a rather difficult one that he would much rather forget if you don't mind.

Ah, Beethoven. How he loves this composer's music. He still can't imagine a more satisfying musical experience than listening to the second and slow movement of his seventh symphony – the part that was used so effectively in that rather good film about King George VI's troublesome speech impediment. Well it moved him before that and even more so when he listened to it in the cinema. Context is everything. He was lucky again that month because he managed to get two tickets for himself and Joan (his compassionate and long-suffering spouse) to hear that very symphony live at the Royal Festival Hall which took them ages to get to by public transport though hardly a long distance as the proverbial crow flies. To be frank, he was moved more by the music heard in his own home than when surrounded by hundreds of musical enthusiasts, some of them slowly guzzling red wine and a few of them audibly masticating crisps and the like. How he hates that. It is not that he considers himself in any way elitist (though he probably is, but that is another issue) but maybe it was more moving when it became a private experience either in his study at home or else when cosily ensconced in the anonymous darkness of the cinema where he is quietly aware of the presence of other people but is unable to actually see them (even though some of them insist on making all kinds of noises). So much for a communal spirit driving collective emotions and the so-called will of the people. He has never been a part of that rather irritating phenomenon though he doesn't deny its power to rally and collectively brainwash vast numbers of normal people. Is this a sad reflection on him?

But that's not the relevant point here, where he is concerned solely with the way in which music can cause spiritual enhancement of the kind that he so desperately needed at that time.

Having immersed himself in the striking musical chords of Beethoven and the supremely satisfying tonal qualities of JS Bach (and by the way his youngest son Johann Christian Bach was a pretty good composer too, though less so than his father), he decided to savour the melodies of other musical geniuses. But however great the composer, we all know that personal preferences hold sway in our enjoyment of music, and you don't have to like great music just because it's so obviously great. It's possible he supposes to appreciate great musical compositions even if one doesn't actually like them. Is that really possible? In his view it is. But that's just him. Is he alone in this? Please tell him he is not alone.

He was entranced by Handel one day, especially by The Messiah, but somewhat less so on the next when he was underwhelmed by some of his operas. The music for the Royal Fireworks transported him to the middle of the eighteenth century with all its extravagant extroversion, but he was also frightened by the cultural alienation that such anachronistic, though magnificent, music induced in his already weakened mental state. No-one can live without Mozart, in his opinion, though he has never been enthralled automatically by every piece of music he wrote with such precision and remarkable speed. But there is no way that he was ever going to listen to all of his forty-one symphonies, though he felt a strange but probably authentic connection with the Jupiter Symphony. He did, however, manage during that month to listen to all of his main operas, and was deeply moved by several arias of The Magic Flute which, in his humble view, is the greatest of all his operas. During one of these, where Pamina in Act Two contemplates suicide, he found the shared emotions almost unbearable. But the overall effect was still a good one. That was very fortunate.

He knows the world of music is endless but that doesn't stop him from listening to it strategically. He supposes even now that he can only scratch the surface of all the compositions that have ever been written but he is only human, after all (so far as we know), so he just has to be selective in what he chooses. Of course, we all have our favourite pieces, some no more than comfort music, but even so that is probably enough for one person and especially for this one purpose that is his obsession. It's odd as he has always felt that a verbal and technical description of a piece of music just doesn't truly convey the nature of the musical experience itself. He perceives a curious but definite dissociation between the official text, however technically accurate, and the sounds that enter his nervous system. One day he might actually understand the differences between modal and tonal music, as well as the nature of diatonic scales, melody and harmony. He guesses such terms are grist to the mill for true musical aficionados but they are as clear as mud to Richard. He just wants to enjoy the musical experience rather than study it. The elegiac voice of a Jussi Bjorling, who is in his view, for what it's worth, the king of all tenors, can only be experienced personally to truly appreciate its magic. If only he could have heard his glorious and rather tragic voice in a live concert. He can only dream this unreality.

While his natural inclination is very much in the classical repertoire, he has always had a rather eclectic approach to life, so he also did his best to appreciate some favourite country melodies and popular tunes. Steeleye Span transported him to the darker realms of English folklore while, like many others, he was suitably impressed with the lyrics of Bob Dylan and Leonard Cohen. These afforded some psychological synergy with what he felt most of the time but still made no major inroads into what was even to him a clearly abnormal world view. But it was important to give everyone a fair crack of the whip if he may be allowed to use that rather unfortunate metaphor. He did not ignore the modern classical genre but here he was even more selective as such music has the power to influence and even shock but not to ease his blatantly toxic state of mind. Stravinsky's Rite of

Spring excited him with its hypnotic rhythmic power, but it also had a frightening streak especially when viewed through the focussed and brutal lens of its associated ballet. Perhaps all of these works combined in some mysterious way to provide a sense of unity with the rest of the world. Or perhaps they don't do this to most people. It's impossible to know for certain. That reminds him. There was a medico-legal case that he was involved with when still a young barrister, before he was a QC, where an otherwise healthy middle-aged man suffered a stroke affecting much of the left side of his brain which severely impaired his speech which was almost unintelligible. The expert neurologists naturally gave completely opposing views of the likely cause of the poor man's catastrophic brain disease, but he was curiously able to sing quite well. He guesses musical appreciation and expression occupies a very special region of the brain, presumably on the right side, or, at least, that is the impression he gleaned from the so-called experts whom he assumed knew what they are talking about. But, of course, he is not a doctor or a scientist. At the end of the month he again managed to get quite expensive tickets for a concert which included Ralph Vaughn Williams's Fifth Symphony. Even though he is easily his favourite British composer he tried to listen as if he were hearing the music for the first time. As you will know this is an extremely difficult thing to do but he tried it anyway. The sublime slow third movement played gentle havoc with his innermost emotions even more than usual, and for the first and only time that February he thought the future might be worth living through after all. That's what great music does.

CHAPTER 4

March - A gastronomic experience

He has never underestimated the power of food. This whole subject has become remarkably popular over the last ten years or so and he is not in the slightest bit surprised that it has. After all, as his late mother always used to tell him, 'You are what you eat' and she had a point; though this kind of maxim is obviously far too simplistic to be literally true. Since he wanted to experience more keenly the influence of physical taste on his general mood during this month, it made sense to focus on what he eats both in the home and in public places such as restaurants. But there must also be a more subtle relationship between our general health and what we shove into our mouths rather than just the physical consequences of conditioning and pleasure (he hopes he's not sounding too much like a judge here as that is not his intention at all). He is thinking of the quite recently appreciated link between the brain and the gut which he has heard some experts encapsulate in the catchy phrase 'The gut is a person's second brain'. He can certainly see what they mean by this and where this concept might lead to even though he is just a layman, though in virtue of his very profession he is meant to be well above average intelligence. Maybe he is but there is nothing about high intelligence that either guarantees sanity or precludes stupidity; he should know, otherwise he would not be thinking along these lines right now.

He thinks there is something very real about the close link between the gut and the brain. But it's probably also a very complex relationship. Everyday experience tells us that must be the case. If he is nervous for some reason before a major case brought before him in Court (and yes Judges get nervous too believe it or not) then he suffers painful spasms in his abdomen for hours afterwards even though he has made sure that there was no outward sign of his distress that anyone else might detect. When he was a child this problem was far worse. Don't tell me you haven't experienced this as well. The brain sends out a distress call and the gut responds with a spasm from hell. But that's a fairly trivial example. His medical and scientific colleagues tell him there is also something they call the 'microbiome' which is the name they give to the vast numbers, he thinks literally trillions, of microbes that inhabit all our bodies, particularly the gut, which are vitally important in maintaining our well-being.

These microbes, mainly bacteria, help us digest food and protect us from the harmful effects of nasty invading organisms. Well, there's a thought. If something goes wrong with the composition of our microbiome then, because of their important widespread effects on the rest of the body including the brain, then we can get ill, possibly very ill. Anyway, that's the gist of it. He hopes he has that broadly right. The important point is that the gut and the brain strongly influence each other so what we put into our mouths as food and drink does not just have the importance of maintaining our nutrition and in some instances giving pleasure to our overworked taste buds. It's all rather simple really when you think about it. But do our taste buds know all this? Probably not.

So much for the science. What about the effect all this gastronomic pleasure has on his dark outlook on life? Before getting to that, he has to recall all the bad things about taste. There's the notion of 'bad taste' for a start which of course has absolutely nothing to do with our taste buds but everything to do with good manners, appropriate aesthetics and etiquette. He reckons that's something that is learned rather than coming naturally and here it can border on snobbery. He should know, having seen all of this first hand especially when he was making his way to the so-called top when he worked excessively hard as an up and coming young barrister trying to climb up the greasy proverbial ladder to success. Then there is the metaphor of something unpleasant that one has witnessed (his legal training coming to the fore again there) or heard about leaving a 'bad taste' in the mouth. What on earth has that got to do with the actual sensation of taste? Absolutely nothing. Then there is the genuinely bad taste where what we put in our mouths to eat is so indescribably foul that we declare that it tastes awful and may even need to be spat out (directly as a child and using a napkin as an adult which he suspect happens more frequently than we think). He has had plenty of those kinds of unpleasant experiences at formal dinners and similar events which are enough to put one off eating altogether were it not for the annoying sense of hunger that compels us to eat. And sometimes when we are really ravenously hungry, we tend to eat so fast that we end up bolting our food and not tasting anything at all. What a waste of a potentially good culinary sensation. Even worse, we British are so meek we seldom complain about awful meals.

So, we finally come to food itself and he spent a good deal of last March, about three times a week on average, eating out with his wife Joan at a whole variety of different London restaurants, some pretty reasonably priced while others were exorbitant and in more than just a few cases a total rip-off. These restaurant owners were taking the piss out of their customers, to coin a phrase if he may, and laughing all the way to the bank. But here he reveals even more of his innate prejudices against so-called fine dining which is a term that invariably irritates him to the point of distraction (though distraction of course was the one thing he was really looking for at that troubled time). That surely was the whole point.

Sometimes, as he has said before, he can get confused by the labour of his own thinking.

Of course, it is a truism, known by just about everyone, that the enjoyment of food is intimately dependent on the circumstances in which it is eaten. Eating alone can be a joyless, even painful experience, whereas sharing a delicious meal with convivial company, including family and friends, possibly enhanced by a glass or two of good red or white wine, can be truly life-enhancing. The only difference between these two very different scenarios is the presence or absence of people. He has been fortunate in that he has experienced countless meals in top restaurants because of his relatively high position, not to mention his comparatively, but not excessively, high salary, and even with his retired Judge's pension he fully accepts that he is far better off that the vast majority of the population. He is privileged for sure in that regard. Unfortunately, together with, or perhaps caused by, that very privileged state, Richard is also suicidal. That's his problem and the question was whether there were enough good things happening around him to make him feel differently about things. At that particular time about nine months ago he was still sceptical about a good outcome. Incidentally, he has a conflicting view about wine. He thinks he can always tell the difference very quickly between a bad wine and a good one. But he doubts he is very adept at distinguishing between a good bottle of wine and an extremely good one that might cost at least ten times as much. He has never had time for that kind of alcoholic snobbery, and he has never been convinced that restaurants are not cynically ripping off its customers with their ridiculous mark ups. How they get away with it he is at a loss to understand. His guess is that it may have a lot to do with one-upmanship and the desire to impress one's colleagues with these florid and absurd displays of wealth. The Emperor's new clothes syndrome in his opinion and it all ends up with everyone pulling the wool over the eyes of everyone else. He has lived a long time and seen this many times. It causes his blood to boil and his temper to fray. As for the sheer absurdity of so-called 'nouveau cuisine' in which the poor customer is forced to pay a small fortune for a miniscule quantity of food – you know what I mean, with one courgette, a tiny piece of halibut and a few tiny new potatoes – just don't get him going.

You have heard of daylight robbery. Well, he thinks this is evening-heavy robbery. How cynical is it possible to get? The answer is just enough to make the diner pay through the nose. He can't tell you just how angry all this nonsense makes him. But, of course, he doesn't need to tell you as you already know that. In the final analysis, food is just what you need to keep alive. Anything more than that must be viewed as an added bonus.

So then is his mother's pithy saying, *'You are what you eat',* actually true when all things are considered? Yes, of course, he does see in retrospect the partial truth in that over-simplified statement, but he also likes accuracy in all things. And this is not strictly accurate. Whenever witnesses gave their testimony in his Court before him, he always used to get just a little irritated when they were obviously lying or else twisting the truth. Of course, some people get so nervous when giving evidence on oath that their memories become confused or patchy through no real fault of their own. Intent is everything before the law. He suspects he would also have this kind of problem if he were stressed, and indeed intellectually taken apart by clever barristers. And some of these legal characters are seriously clever and good at what they do. But he always did his utmost to put people at their ease whenever he could. Indeed, he had a reputation for personal kindness in the Courtroom which is not that common. After all, he is a person who was almost moved to tears when he witnessed the almost unbearable pathos depicted so vividly in the painting by Jozef Israels called 'The Frugal Meal' (but one must not mix up senses and metaphors). He believes that's a generally held view, but he rather doubts whether more than just a few people either remember him or give a damn about how he operated and why he handed down the sentences he did. But he was pretty severe when he had to be of course, especially with the hardened criminals or child-abusers, but he was never deliberately unfeeling or cold to those unfortunates who were bought before him. Probably through no fault of their own they became further additions to life's tragic no-hopers. He doesn't think of them as losers because a few of these folk somehow, either through good fortune or their own enormous efforts, or sometimes both, manage to rise above the twin dangers of poverty and crime. Such is life, even though it's invariably cruel. If you think he is being cynical and nihilistic then he would plead guilty to both charges. But he digresses, and not for the first time I hear you say. Well he is going to do that a lot so he makes no excuses for it, though he does hope that he is managing at least to provide some explanations as to how he eventually reached his final decision. We shall leave that until very much later. He realises you may not find some, or perhaps all, of his reasoning about this serious matter very convincing in which case all he can say is that it does not actually matter if you do or if you don't because everything he thinks here is the truth and nothing but the truth. His sole aim is to make a sound judgement about the continuation of life based on all the evidence around him from this day and all those days which have gone before. Surely nothing on earth can be as important as that.

CHAPTER 5

April - A touch of class

In many ways the sensation of touch is perhaps the most seductive yet elusive of all the human senses. It embraces a myriad of possibilities, not all of which are immediately obvious or apparent to the conscious individual, but at the same time it affords us undoubted pleasure and is crucial in maintaining our bodily equilibrium and sense of awareness in space. Richard just can't imagine living in a world without being able to touch things or else to be totally untouched.

So how should he begin? Does he start with the mundane experiences of touch or does he revert again to the more imaginative world of metaphors? It would not surprise you to learn that he decided to do both and let his normally precise and ordered mind embrace the vagaries of this most important sense. He means that, in all senses of the word, if that is not a contradiction in terms. He first considered the notion of a 'light touch' which of course has nothing to do with the sensation of touch at all but everything to do with approach and attitude. His response to just about everything and everyone has always been on the light side, though he would prefer to think of himself as more kind and gentle than lightweight. The latter may still leave some kind of physical impression, of course, in virtue of its compressing ability but that has very little to do with his problem of life and death. He would have thought that is perfectly obvious. Nevertheless, he would like to think that he always displayed just a touch of class during his long stint as a high-level English Judge.

If one is touched by something or someone then it follows that one must feel as well, unless one has a neurological disease which impairs the sensation of touch which, so far as he is aware, he does not. Well that's something to be thankful for, he supposes, especially when he thinks about all the wine he must have consumed when he was a young up-and-coming barrister in Lincoln's Inn, intent on gaining success and getting on well with all the right senior people, that is to say, the powerful and well-connected, personal attributes that usually go together. But he knows he really should forget about all that nonsense on the way to the top. Yet somehow, he doesn't think it's possible to entirely separate the sensations of feeling and seeing when it comes to wearing stylish clothes. Not everyone is aware of this but when a Circuit Judge in England and Wales appears at some kind of ceremonial occasion, they wear the most beautiful violet dress robes. He really enjoyed the snug and comfortable feeling of these, especially when the weather was cool, and he liked the elegant appearance of this splendid garb which was much less gaudy and showy than you might think. Perhaps he should not have enjoyed that dressing up so much. But the truth is that he did and considerably so. If he feels comfortable in what he wears, then his whole body is at ease and this must surely be a common phenomenon. I strongly suspect you must have had a similar experience in your own life or work. The truth is that if you dress the part then it's more than likely you will truly feel the part. 'Clothes maketh the man', as his mother always used to tell him. The other thing about dressing up is that it makes it so much easier to play a role. He always tried to do this and one thing he has never doubted is his consummate professionalism, if he says so himself (which of course he knows he shouldn't). Perhaps he may be slightly deranged at this point of his life, but no-one ever criticised him in his professional role. After all, just because something such as work may be pointless, that is certainly no excuse for not carrying on regardless and doing one's job extremely well. That's almost worth writing down somewhere.

To be clear about this, most of the time we are hardly aware of the sense of touch because it just functions as part of our everyday activity and experiences. Speaking frankly (and as you will have already seen, Richard is open and frank here about just about everything) he has considerable difficulty in seeing how touch could have any lasting impact at all on his mood and dark intentions. Except, that is, in extreme circumstances such as when touch causes pain and pleasure. Please don't misunderstand him— he is no masochist. He does not seek painful experiences and fears them greatly both before and after they have happened. The excruciating pain of a burn, however fleeting, or the deep pain of a blow on the knee, elbow or crotch are hell on earth to bear but they probably serve a kind of protective function where one recoils from the possibility of suffering further pain. This thought does not help him in the least and only makes him more terrified of the potentially painful process of dying, especially if botched by one's own hand. That kind of touch will only have a deterrent effect and so in that one sense it has some dubious relevance to his sad predicament.

No, what he seeks is the ability of touch to produce or enhance pleasure since that is potentially something that might actually stay his hand in the hope that the future might promise more of the same kind of experience. And he means much more than everyday pleasures such as the comfortable feeling one gets from wearing well-fitting and stylish clothes or, for that matter, the warm gentle susurrations soothing one's skin in a hot bath or in the Mediterranean ocean.

Perhaps you think he is referring to the pleasures of intimacy and sex, and in that of course you would be quite right. What else could he be referring to? It is, in his view, as much a psychological as a physical pleasure, and much greater than and very different from the undoubted, but transitory, pleasures of fine food and chocolate. He realises the latter can be considerable for many of us, but it can never truly replace the unique sense of mental and physical well-being that often (but sadly not always) results from a truly intimate experience with a loved one, in his case his remarkably attractive and youthful wife, and for others, with a different sexual orientation, some other type of partner. He has never been so stupid or lacking in empathy as to deny the existence of a whole range of different kinds of love– after all, the ancient Greeks had a great deal to say about this (and incidentally he initially read Classics at Oxford before switching to the Law after two years so he thinks he knows what he is talking about).

Anyway, of all the potential reasons for either postponing or permanently discarding his future act of self-destruction, this was for him the most important one. As for the likely effect his sudden death would have on his wife and three children, he can't even imagine how devastating that would be. He may not care much for himself, and it might be a welcome exit from an intrinsically cruel and uncaring world, but he should have no ignorant delusions about how painful such a loss would be to them. It is so easy to underestimate how important one may be to others, especially close family and genuine friends, even when it seems that the rest of life has chewed us up and duly spat us out into a morass of misery and unfairness. So, during the month of April he paid more than his usual minimal attention to Joan, which came as quite a surprise to her, and he felt very much better for several days afterwards. The sad irony is that he looks and acts like a relatively young man, but he feels as if he is as old as Methuselah. He has this strange feeling that he is not alone in this odd yet rather cruel behavioural dichotomy. Have we touched a nerve here?

CHAPTER 6

May - The sweet smell of failure

Smells are evocative. Richard has been aware of this for some time, probably since his youth, and I have no doubt that you also recognise this as one of life's enduring truisms. But his question is why that is the case in both the neurobiological and the emotional sense. Of course, he realises these two ways of looking at this fact of nature may ultimately stem from the same underlying process and be the end result of the interactions of vast numbers of neural pathways within our brains. Now there's a thought. Though he is just a layman he does read popular medicine and science books from time to time and has also learned quite a lot from the various expert medical witnesses who have testified before him throughout his judicial career. Some of them spoke nervously, others authoritatively, and some displayed both aspects of their character which was usually, but not always, one of considerable distinction. So, he is not a complete medical ignoramus. You must have realised that some time ago. So far as he understands it from these experts, the sense of smell is picked up by specialised structures within the nasal cavity (now there's a surprise) from where the nervous pathways pass through the skull and finally end up in a part of the brain called the olfactory cortex in the frontal lobes of the brain. Some smell-mediated pathways also end up in a structure called the hippocampus which rests snugly within the temporal lobe of the brain.

Nature is so clever, or maybe the process of natural selection is the clever one. He thinks that because the temporal lobe is where memory is processed, so both the sense of smell and one's personal memory are processed, and so he assumes, are associated with each other, in the same part of the brain. So that must be why he thinks automatically of dreadful school dinners and strict unsympathetic school teachers whenever he is assailed by the sickly smell of cheap mashed potatoes and spam. And he still remembers being literally traumatised by the spectre of semolina. How he feared that desert. A rather more pleasant association is the unmistakable smell of wood polished with beeswax that will always remind him of the elegant combination room in his old Oxford College where fellows and their guests used to congregate just before dining at High Table. He always enjoys the subtle fragrance of his wife's favourite perfume but also remembers the loathing and fear that the clawing perfume of one of his aunts always used to produce. Perhaps it is as simple as that. Actually, it is incredibly complex and requires many billions of nerve cells, each one of which connects via thousands of synapses with vast numbers of other nerve cells. He is seldom in awe of anything, but he is for sure in awe of the indescribably complicated structure and working of the human brain. It has the same effect on him as does contemplation of the Universe, but we will deal with that one later. Patience is a virtue, one which he knows he has always lacked. But these unusual but consistent associations between smell and the vivid recollection of events have also been inspirational for many generations of writers and philosophers. But how does all this help him? He is not certain it does. In fact, it doesn't. It is interesting though for sure.

Smells are also underestimated. They can serve so many useful as well as useless purposes. They can give us a jolt which stops the sleepyheads nodding off while driving which was more than useful when his father used to drive his teenage children across the Swiss Alps. That was a stressful experience for everyone. He first became aware of his intrinsic aggression and power to loathe when he witnessed this act of self-preservation. But the strength of that memory is still not powerful enough to deliver him from an impending act of self-destruction. He remembers the sulphurous reek of stink bombs as a schoolboy which seem so rare these days and the vicious physical punishments such acts of childish obscenity invariably invoked. Recalling those again brings out his latent capacity to hate authority even though, ironically, he was to become part of a high-level authoritative infrastructure himself. As to the equally sulphurous, if not volcanic, fumes that sometimes emanate from unfortunate people with a certain type of digestion, or, more accurately, indigestion, curiously he confesses to a strange feeling of compassion far more often than revulsion at this accidental outpouring of offensive effluence. So he really can't be that bad as a person, can he? You, and not I, must be the judge of that when all is told.

He then tried a further mental manoeuvre, one that was more akin perhaps to a sort of retrospective thought experiment. Scientists do this all the time, though more in relation to the future and the unknown as we know, but in Richard's case he was doing it primarily to seek a form of personal salvation. He tried hard to think of the most enjoyable and evocative experiences he could that also involved the sense of smell. He wanted to use this memory to enhance the current enjoyment of life assuming that was even possible. So, on one rainy Sunday in May he sat down on the most comfortable armchair in his study in his North London house and, lightly closing his eyes, tried hard to think of holidays, something that always makes him feel good. He forced his mind into a settled blankness and let the memories slowly form. He quite suddenly became aware of the most delicious and unmistakable smell of breakfast in one of the many guesthouses he and Joan had stayed in over the previous twenty years. It was comprised presumably of the smells of a classic 'full English' (how he dislikes that phrase, but still...), with cooked sausages, bacon and eggs and coffee and just for a moment he was transported to the stylish cosiness of an upmarket hotel in Northern England. He knows from some of the cases he has ruled on that some unfortunate people experience this kind of smell as a result of an unusual type of seizure (that's epilepsy to you and me) but that was, most emphatically, not true in his case as he had deliberately conjured up this vivid and extremely pleasant act of odiferous recall, and it certainly did not just appear spontaneously. Many of the most enjoyable moments of one particular visit to this beautiful countryside gently permeated his consciousness and he experienced a comparatively rare frisson of mental and physical pleasure. But he was not altogether successful in this mental effort as he was just unable to hold onto this vision for more than a few seconds. He then tried to do the same thing again but failed totally. For a few seconds his mind managed to reach as far back as his childhood when his father took him to a delicatessen in the South of France, when the pleasant but pungent smell of Camembert cheese struck him as soon as they walked through the makeshift door made of several strings of hanging beads. But that pleasurable memory also evaporated just a few seconds after it appeared and then his recall would function no more. Overall, he would have given himself an A for effort and B minus for sustained success.

Later that month he decided instead to immerse himself in real smells of a pleasant nature, so he decided to pay a long overdue visit to the magnificent Kew Gardens in South-west London. If he was to be impressed with the sight and smells of a myriad of plants and flowers, then surely this is where it would most likely happen. He had always had a close affinity with the striking red, pink, yellow and white rhododendrons that appeared in full bloom at this time of the year, especially in our national parks and private gardens, but he was keen to smell floral beauty itself as his principal task for the month of May.

With this aim in mind he arrived at the Royal Botanic Gardens one Thursday morning late in the month for the first time in over thirty years, a delay which was far too long. How many times do all of us have that feeling of regret when eventually returning to a National jewel like this? The place is vast, and even had its own small police force, the Kew Constabulary, and so he needed to be focussed in what was explored. All of us are constantly being told about the need for 'focus' in our work, especially in science, but in his humble view, such as it is, the truly rounded and wise person has the capacity to be focussed like a laser beam when the circumstances demand yet at the same time be able to see the broad overall picture. As a Judge, that dual ability is of critical importance if the wisest possible ruling is to emerge. But he must be more focussed and stop these constant digressions.

It was impossible for him to explore in just one day the Garden's entire repertoire of plant houses, elegant ornamental buildings, galleries, museums, Kew Palace, plant collections, exquisite flowers and much else besides. He was literally overwhelmed by the impressive historical provenance of many of these exhibits, all laid out in perfect harmony for the discerning visitor. So, what did he do? He was a man with a mission, as you can imagine, so he made a beeline for any area of the gardens that attracted him because of its colour and physical beauty in the hope that would lead him to the sweetest smelling of the plants and flowers. This was his strategy, perhaps just a little perverse in its mode of execution, and he spent many hours of the day surreptitiously sniffing every single plant, tree, flower and building in order to somehow allow these experiences to energise and infiltrate his darkening mood, one that had showed no sign of improvement despite all his best efforts. He must have looked like either a complete madman or a somewhat eccentric plant enthusiast, or maybe more likely in the current liberal-minded times a curious but benign mixture of both. He also thought there was just a hint of the canine about the way in which he conducted himself.

So, what were the flowers that gave him the greatest nasal hit? Well frankly he was unable to recall all their names, but if he included those sniffed both in the magnificent Gardens and in his own neighbourhood, he could identify the sweet-smelling lilacs, the sweet peas climbing up the garage in his own back garden, white jasmine, freesias, magnolias, the ubiquitous divine-smelling roses, gardenias, scented primroses, viburnums, honeysuckles (which caused him to sneeze uncontrollably), and hyacinths. He was sure there must be very many more, perhaps even more odiferous, but these experiences did a lot to stabilise his mood and give him a strong sense of mental equilibrium. Thus comforted, at least for a while by these extremely agreeable sensations, he must have made at least a modicum of progress even if he had to wait much later for the proverbial quantum leap.

CHAPTER 7

June - The grandeur all around us

So far, Richard had concentrated his attention on the five principal human senses, namely sight, hearing, taste, touch and smell in the hope that he might derive some measure of inspiration and optimism for the continuation of his life. Those first few months of his somewhat macabre experiment had turned out rather better than he had at first anticipated, and at the very least he had been given a degree of hope for the future. But there is also a sixth sense that belongs to humans and we are not referring here to that strange, if not mystical, intuitive sense that sometimes allows us to make informed guesses in certain situations that turn out to be unnervingly correct. No, he meant something quite different. He was thinking of our aesthetic sense, one which, perhaps uniquely among all animal species, gives us the ability to appreciate the beauty and grandeur that exists almost everywhere in the natural world, assuming we have the right mindset to appreciate it and the will to seek it out wherever it exists. So, during the month of June he decided to explore and hopefully gain some solace from an active appreciation of this unique feature of the world around us.

He realised of course that an appreciation of our natural surroundings requires more than just one of our senses. The capacity to see reality before us is an obvious *sine qua non* but what he wanted to experience was something rather different than just what was pleasing to the eye. He was seeking a more spiritual experience in which visual beauty alone was a necessary but certainly not sufficient requirement for what was meant. In some magical way there somehow needed to be an underlying *frisson* of mental charge that could penetrate deeply and meaningfully into his emotional state and make a real difference. But to achieve this, the mind needs to prepare itself, perhaps unconsciously, in an open and relaxed manner so that it can be properly receptive to the notion of grandeur and beauty. That's easier said than done.

For sure, he had been impressed with the multicoloured and ubiquitous rhododendrons that were most striking in May, and which were still elegant in June, yet this is a good example of striking beauty without the more powerful creation of awe. It was a charming visual experience, but it just lacked the depths he so desperately sought.

So, he decided to visit mountains, lakes, the coast and the ocean, knowing that the British Isles has a vast repertoire of all of these essential ingredients of natural beauty, ones that were sublime and magisterial in equal measure. But where was he to start such a survey? There seemed to be so much to choose from. After a good deal of careful thought, he decided to begin close to home and then work his way upwards towards the North. He has always been quite a logical and orderly person and he felt his simple strategy aptly reflected this. Living in London meant that he could reach the South Coast in less than two hours by train, his favourite mode of public transport. After reaching Victoria station from his home in the north of the capital city, he soon found himself walking briskly along the extensive sea front of Eastbourne, a seaside town of considerable charm and prolonged sunshine, and also one whose quality, in his view, has always been generally underestimated. He could see the coastline melding into the calm sea stretching for several miles in each direction, a blue and golden vista of ocean and sand that reinforced the notion of both the passage of undulating time and a strange form of restless tranquillity. He could easily have just stayed for hours on end standing in just one point along the promenade through some kind of powerful inertia, but instead walked along and explored almost everything within his vision. Here and there it was possible to make out the hazy outlines of small boats gently bobbing along far out to sea while nearer to home were surprisingly few bathers, some just testing the waters, so to speak, with their feet in this rather cool summer day while others, perhaps more bravely, were swimming tentatively within several metres from the sandy beach. Throughout this time he was fully aware of the endless tour buses containing enthusiastic and interested sightseers, many rather elderly, the long and enormous pier jutting far out into the sea, boasting a range of entertainment and an elegant restaurant, and, of course, the whole place dominated by the magisterial spectre of the chalk headland of Beachey Head, with its steep cliffs promising great views and beauty but from which many desperate and miserable people over the years had deliberately jumped to their deaths. One thing he knew for sure that day was that he was not going to be one of them, at least not on that occasion and almost certainly not in that brutal manner. The very sight and thought made him shiver. He was not that disillusioned with life after all. He was just in the assessment phase, as it were.

That was a good start, but more emotional stimulation was required. So, he spent the next two weeks of the month wandering further afield. From Eastbourne he ventured all along England's South Coast, exploring to the East the coastal town of Hastings which he knew well with its impressive cliffs, funicular railways, characterful 'retro' shops reminiscent of the idiosyncratic nineteen-seventies, historic buildings reflecting its distinguished maritime history, and shingle beach leading to the sea. Further eastwards and very nearby, he also paid a visit to the exquisite town of Rye with its cobbled streets, strikingly elegant medieval, half-timbered houses, impressive castle and museum, reportedly haunted hotel, and, coursing across one's lower vision in the distance, the deceptively benign Romney Marsh. He also journeyed Westward to sample again the delights of the Dorset coast. This he knew less well as a staunch Londoner, but was more than impressed with the sheer beauty and liveability of Weymouth with its genuinely sandy beach, invigorating sea air, and abundant ice cream stalls, and then the nearby Isle of Portland where he saw a veritable flotilla of sailing boats emerging from the man-made harbour, the Jurassic Coast, where he experienced the strange graduated allure of Chesil Beach, viewed in the distance the upper and lower lighthouses, and became vividly aware of the town's enormous strategic importance during wartime. He did not, however, have any desire to view its two prisons. On the journey back eastwards he paid a brief visit to the coastal town of Bournemouth where he was duly impressed with the abundant Victorian architecture and realised that it would probably be a good place to live especially if his aim was to reach one hundred years; though frankly, this was the last thing he intended to do. The final place Richard saw was the forward-thinking city of Brighton which seemed to him to be very similar to his home city of London in many ways, and almost as expensive with its elegant shops, Regency houses and Georgian terraces, but far more manageable somehow and, critically, it was by the coast which was, after all, the key object of the whole exercise. He also had the impression that there were a lot of happy people there. But you can understand that he was the very last person qualified to be a judge of peoples' mood; a Judge of their behaviour and actions perhaps but not of their souls. So, his somewhat eccentric quest for emotional enlightenment by exploring the sea and the coast had succeeded in part, but it was also necessary to see what effect natural beauty on a grander, greater scale might produce.

The second half of June was, therefore, devoted to a journey far north of London. Again, there was an obvious requirement for focus given the vast possibilities that Britain has to offer. There were two places that were pre-eminent in his mind, and if these did not have a life-enhancing effect then he was in little doubt that no-where else would. Both regions were familiar to him, though it had been several years since he had visited either. On this occasion his wife Joan accompanied him, not only because, to be honest, he just wanted her to, a feeling that he was pleased to say was warmly reciprocated, but also because in his experience it is always a good idea to share a powerful emotional experience with another person, preferably a loved one, because in some mysterious way, that closeness has the capacity to magnify all that is good in the world. Maybe he is a romantic after all.

Much as if he were trying to mimic the attempted challenge of the mythical Norse God Thor, he first imagined himself drinking water from a goblet that was in fact supplied from the waters of Lake Derwent, one of many strange illusions this iconic jewel of the Lake District created in his mind as he gazed from a height at the shiny interface between water and land. This outlandish analogy had an element of truth in one sense, only which is that he would not have been able to take in the sheer beauty of the Lake District in its entirety, even after a multitude of visits. Sometimes a vista is so compelling in its beauty that it is just not possible to crystallise its whole essence or the feelings it induces in just a few words, however well chosen. William Wordsworth, the remarkable poet of the Lakes, managed many aspects of this near impossible task better than anyone else of course, but Richard's sensibilities must clearly be somewhat inferior as when confronted with the overwhelming tranquillity of seemingly endless, though somehow connected, rustic brown mountains, green rolling hills, silver coated lakes and azure sky, all he could do was look on rather mindlessly and try to observe the sights as best he could. Words seldom fail him, as you may possibly have noticed, but when clambering up these classic slopes they sometimes did. That, though, was both the problem and the whole point of the exercise.

Equally attractive in their own way were the chocolate box cottages and also grander houses that could be discerned with some clarity from high up on the mountains on a clear day, dispersed with elegant irregularity and randomness between steep vistas of mountains and grass. How enjoyable and comfortable it would have been to actually live permanently in these, from a distance, picturesque dwellings he still does not know, but he had little doubt that it would be as exciting as it might also be physically and mentally demanding. He may be indescribably impressed with the lure of the countryside but at heart he was still a city dweller, and always has been. Visiting and living in a place are quite separate activities. It is as well for us all to be aware of that delusion and not get trapped in a bucolic dream which is just that. A dream in all its unreality.

But from such dreams it is possible to derive inspiration and, in this sense, alone those few days spent in Cumbria in Northern England lived up to all their expectations, and very much more. During that week he experienced several other iconic sights and locations within what he still thinks as rural fairyland

and now fully understands why some people he knows insist on visiting the Lake District at least once per year. Perhaps they feel it's good for the soul.

He would certainly agree with that rather mystical view, but for certain it did considerably more than that in his sad case. But he was not yet quite finished with the closeness of mountains and water. How could he not revisit the Highlands of Scotland?

As they walked along the well-worn pathways looking down on the shores of Lake Torridon, deep within the region of Wester Ross in the Western Highlands of Scotland, the perception of a curiously isolated tranquillity was the predominant emotion they both experienced.

Perhaps under the unusual circumstances, that was the most useful gift this rugged mountainous landscape could give to a still troubled mind. It was still so difficult for him to separate cause from effect. Did his abnormal mental state determine how he reacted to such magnificent countryside or did the landscape itself truly re-awaken a powerful but dormant ability to appreciate beauty? And does the answer to this question really matter? Probably not – what is evident to the senses just is. Its true origin is surely irrelevant. You must judge.

He was convinced the weather has a vital role to play in determining mood. But, somewhat paradoxically, both of these regions of outstanding natural beauty that had such a beneficial effect on his psyche, generally have a very wet climate with grey skies and only intermittent sunshine. Far from deterring people like him, this curious dissociation of bad weather and alluring landscape serves to highlight just how impressive and indeed addictive these places must be. Above all it is vital to be fair in all matters, and this includes the assessment of the quality of life everywhere and that includes what to city folk regard as isolated pockets of great beauty. That said, he was convinced they were both extremely cyclothymic individuals, especially himself, by which he meant that they are greatly affected by the seasons with bright sunshine causing an almost automatic elevation of mood, while continuous rain invariably produces the opposite effect. But surely any truly well-balanced individual would have the capacity to carry on with life and whatever else they are doing irrespective of the local weather? Is this yet another example of what Richard is increasingly beginning to suspect is a mental illness? But perhaps the very fact that he is able to ask this question so honestly signifies that he is perfectly sane. Now that's a difficult one to be sure.

CHAPTER 8

July - The magnificent structures humans build

Richard had spent virtually the whole month of June trying his very best to appreciate and be stimulated by the natural beauty of the countryside. He had succeeded in part but what he next set out to do during July was view, contemplate and maybe even judge, a hand-picked sample of the world's most impressive man-made structures. Now that is what can be called a tall order. But it is not altogether inaccurate as many of the places he decided to see or at least think about were physically massive, though he was clear in his own mind that size alone was not to be the only criterion that he would apply in attributing his particular notion of greatness. That is another contradiction in terms, but in his current state surely he can be allowed a few of these.

He decided to focus on magnificent places of worship such as cathedrals, imposing architecture, both in the current and previous centuries, and superhuman examples of engineering including great bridges, railways and dams. Why did he choose these? The answer may seem a little trite, but something within his rather eccentric (not twisted) psyche was convinced that if he could be totally captivated by the intrinsic greatness of the achievements of his fellow humans throughout history, then somehow that would encourage him to want to remain a living member of the human species. He realised the logic of that view is difficult to appreciate, and even now with hindsight it does seem a bit ridiculous, if not pretentious. But at the same time, it is essential to realise that this represents the whole truth of what he felt and how things developed. Sometimes truth and logic are not the same and can even be at the opposite ends of the spectrum. Be that as it may, this is what took place.

He started with places of worship even though he was a staunch agnostic. There is no contradiction there because, as we shall see later, this view of God and the world is almost certainly the most logical. The fact that many generations of mankind have built truly magnificent edifices to glorify the notion, and for them the reality, of God, and allow people to worship there, is surely a completely natural aspect, indeed consequence, of the eternal human spirit. He frankly did not care very much about the true motivation for building great cathedrals and churches. What he did care about is what the architects and builders actually achieved and the end result. He would describe that as a pragmatic approach to the appreciation of religious buildings. He hopes this does not make him seem just a trifle arrogant. He is not.

Some of the great man-made edifices he had already witnessed, some many years previously, a few others he decided to see for himself to take in their stature first hand, while others still were so far away in distant lands that the most he could do was imagine or read everything he could about them. What he could not experience directly he would need to reconstruct in his mind. He had been to forty-five different countries during his lifetime but that is still only a quarter of the total possible, and, as you know, no-one can do the impossible. Remarkably, he had never before set foot inside the great St Paul's Cathedral on Ludgate Hill in East London though he had often seen its inimitable dome dominating the skyline from a distance. So often a city's long-term inhabitants never bother to see its greatest architectural treasures, and Richard was no exception to that universal truism. But he was not alone in perpetrating this common act of civil laziness. So, he took the underground tube to the appropriately named St Paul's station and walked the short distance to Sir Christopher Wren's great masterwork (though his assistant, the great architect Nicholas Hawksmoor, also had something to do with the design). At 365 feet high the Cathedral is still the highest point of the city of London (a fact that he did know at least) and it also houses the Bishop of London. He entered the magisterial building and spent about an hour there, suitably impressed with the Cathedral's great Dome. He was thrilled and energised by what he saw, and it made him keen to see more of the same. Was he not satisfied with grandeur on this scale? Apparently not as his next port of call that day was none other than Westminster Abbey, the great gothic Abbey Church that used to be a Cathedral in the sixteenth century. He knew it had hosted numerous coronations and

Royal weddings and, most moving of all, it also housed the tomb of the 'Unknown Soldier'. He entered with enthusiasm and came out suitably humbled.

As a teenager, fifty years before, he had visited both Lincoln and Durham Cathedrals but had little memory of either masterpiece. But this time as an adult he only had the will to visit Lincoln, largely because the alluring vision of steep roads, both elegant and narrow and bounded by charming houses around the Cathedral had always stayed with him. So, one sunny morning in the first week of July he took the train from London to the historic town of Lincoln and before long the striking vision of the medieval gothic Cathedral stood before him, proud and magnificent. The interior was every bit as evocative as the outside vision promised and he was more than impressed that it also housed one of only four surviving copies of Magna Carta, the historic thirteenth-century charter of rights signed by the particularly unpleasant King John at Runnymede. That's the kind of historical artefact that somehow puts almost everything into a sharp perspective. As you can imagine that ancient document had a very particular resonance for him as a professional lawyer.

That is what he had hoped for more than anything at the time. He did not have the energy to revisit Durham Cathedral with its famous Norman architecture even though he had a vague recollection that it had once impressed him more than any of them. He did, however, later that week, pay a short visit to Canterbury Cathedral in Kent, which was not that far from London, but he had difficulty in trying to imagine that the Archbishop Thomas Beckett was murdered within its confines in 1170. Fortunately, no such fate is ever likely to end the life of the present Archbishop of Canterbury. But again, it was the powerful historical jolt that these places produced that most affected him. The only other similar liturgical occasion that had moved him to this extent was his first appreciation of the extraordinary beauty of Florence Cathedral (the *Duomo di Firenze* in Italian), with its green and white exterior and famous Dome designed by Filippo Brunelleschi in the fifteenth century. That had been a truly spiritual experience and even the distant recall of a place devoted to God many centuries before was enough to impress him greatly in retrospect. You do not have to believe in either God or, for that matter, any religion at all, to be in genuine awe of the Duomo.

So much for Cathedrals and Churches, great testaments to man's creative abilities as they undoubtedly were. But he needed to see more to be absolutely sure. An interesting insight he gained from all the great buildings he had visited so far had been a strong sense of symmetry at every level. Assuming that is truly important in our appreciation of grandeur, symmetry is also thought by many to be a key component of physical beauty in humans, male and female alike, so perhaps there is something universally attractive about that particular characteristic.

Great Dams had always had a powerful effect on him. It is not so much their sheer size that works the magic, though that must certainly be an important element in their strange fascination, but more the great potential danger people tend to perceive when they see them. He worries about the twin perils of injury or death during their construction and the ever-present theoretical risk of the Dam bursting. Maybe he has just seen too many war films.

Though he has never actually seen the famous Hoover Dam, the massive water-preventing concrete structure between Nevada and Arizona located in the Black Canyon of the Colorado River (which he had seen many years ago), pictures of this iconic Dam still filled him with an unsettling combination of admiration and fear. And so he was not surprised to learn that during its five-year construction more than one hundred workers died. That is a lot of dead workers.

The planning and sheer effort of construction involved was truly remarkable to be sure, and it seemed to him that no one person was responsible for its success. Rather, it was created by a vast team at every level of seniority and responsibility. That was a realisation of great significance because what he was seeking was evidence of human ingenuity rather than the brilliance of just one person. He experienced a similar sense of unbridled wonder when he confronted the Petronas Twin Towers in Kuala Lumpur. How living people managed to construct these towers, which reached a height of 1483 feet, not to mention the sky bridge connecting them, remained a complete mystery to him. As for what is currently the tallest building in the world, the extraordinary Burj Khalifa in Dubai standing at 2722 feet, which he had also seen, words failed him. It was so difficult for him to get his head around the effort and brilliance necessary to build these massive structures. Sometimes great power and elegance combine in a more immediate fashion, as he always thought was the case with the remarkable Art Deco-style Chrysler Building in New York. But his attitude towards these extraordinary skyscrapers might have been different had he not read William Golding's dark novel 'The Spire'. That tale addressed many aspects of human behaviour but to him above all else it warned of the dangers of trying to build too high. The tallest building may for some people reach out nearer to God, but for him it also brought us nearer to extinction.

Then he thought about individual prowess in engineering, so of course his mind wandered back to the nineteenth century to the great engineer Isambard Kingdom Brunel. He reckoned with a name like that he must have been a genius. How he managed to build all he did before he died at the age of fifty-three years is extraordinary, though many geniuses in the physical sciences and mathematics tend to do most of their great work while still young. Lawyers, by contrast, rather like physicians and classicists, tend to improve with age, like good red wine or Port. Once you have a talent for something, like bridge construction or railway creation, as Brunel clearly had, then you just keep going and do the same kind of thing over and over again. He was thinking especially of his Clifton Suspension Bridge spanning the Avon

Gorge in Bristol, The Thames Tunnel, the Great Western Railway, and also the largest ship ever built in 1843, not to mention his numerous other bridges. While we are on the subject of bridges, as a Londoner, he was, naturally, very aware of the modern London Bridge, a concrete and steel box girder construction, which is one of our great landmarks with an extensive history, mainly but not completely good. He had also seen and walked across the Humber Bridge, an exceptionally long suspension bridge spanning the Humber estuary. He had not seen the Forth Bridge, a cantilever bridge spanning the Firth of Forth but was suitably impressed by its vision and historic provenance. As for the iconic Sydney Bridge, the steel arch bridge which he had once seen with his own eyes many years ago, all he could do then is remember, think, and wonder. He views it now as a true gateway to the imagination even more than as a bridge straddling a great harbour. His overall conclusion at the end of July was that all these magnificent man-made structures more than amply passed the stringent test he had so arrogantly set them. So, the month ended well.

CHAPTER 9

August - Food for thought

There was not a great deal for him, or for that matter anyone, to do that August being in the midst of the so-called 'silly season' where everyone seems to be away on vacation and nothing of any real importance seems to get done. Therefore, he decided to spend the month thinking, always a rather dangerous and potentially subversive thing to do in any age. He knew that life was not as good as it could have been, given what should have been a great sense of freedom from the traumas of the legal workplace. But that of course was his underlying problem. By consulting the writings of some of our great philosophers he kept alive the forlorn hope that somewhere in their profound thoughts he might find some degree of inspiration that might help his plight. Anyway, that was the general idea.

It was obvious to Richard that he was suffering a great deal from a sense of alienation, of being cut off from the workplace, of being alone in the world despite the presence of his family. While there is, he realised, a definite element of self-indulgence, if not pity, in that situation, nevertheless it was real enough to him and at least he was trying to do something about it and find a remedy, even though he recognised then, and even more so now, that his approach to the problem was just a trifle eccentric. But what is wrong with a bit of eccentricity? After all, most people can be pretty boring when they really try hard. There is nothing perverse about being eccentric. But if people perceive that you are original rather than eccentric, then they have the capacity to hate you for it. After all, no good turn goes unpunished. He should know.

As an undergraduate, many years ago, he had read many of the key works of some of the great philosophers, especially those in antiquity, but he needed an urgent refresher course even though he managed to retain a smattering of philosophical knowledge. Intrinsically, he found all philosophy to be extremely difficult to get his head round. In fact, the more he read of it then the greater the difficulty became because he began to realise the inherent complexity of the subject. But whether it is true that bad philosophy is probably not philosophy at all, as the late philosopher and novelist Iris Murdoch once stated, he was just unable to say. But she was probably right. The problem as he saw it was that he perceived two different worlds, namely the world of work and the world of not working, and if one is defined by one's work then there is a real danger of becoming alienated from the whole world when work ceases to be the main focus in life. But that is a limited view of the world even though it was real enough for Richard. He immediately thought of the main philosophical work of the great German philosopher Martin Heidegger, called Being and Time (originally *Sein und Zeit* in the original German). His work is notoriously difficult to read and understand but he was deeply struck by his existentialist notion of what he called *Dasein* which, as he understood it, means existence in so far as everyone is conceptualised as 'Being-in-the world', which is the basic state of *Dasein*. We do most things mechanically without really thinking about our existence *per se* but that situation changes when something new or unexpected has an effect on this unconscious state of being. He thought this was a clear and original way of viewing existence and, of course, Heidegger constructed a vast edifice of philosophical analysis based on and extending the notion of *Dasein*, one which was a critical forerunner of the modern existentialist movement. But while this view of Being-in-the world, as he put it in his inimitable and idiosyncratic way, helped Richard greatly to understand what existence in the real world as it is might comprise, it had no ethical implications and it made his own notion, which was completely different and far less subtle, seem superficial and lacking in intellectual force. But at least it clarified what he thought he meant. In fact, he was no longer certain of exactly what he meant by existence in two worlds. But even if his conception was flawed it didn't unfortunately change his unhinged mindset one jot.

But Heidegger was not exactly a very nice chap even though he was clearly a genius. After all, he was reported to be a Nazi sympathiser which virtually all of us would condemn as utterly beyond the pale. But does it matter? Is it possible to dissociate the man's moral stance from his philosophy? Wagner was another genius – a truly great composer for sure – who was also morally flawed in that he was by all accounts anti-Semitic. That is a form of racism that he found particularly abhorrent, not only because Richard had an element of Jewish heritage a few generations back, but also because it seems to embody everything that is truly evil in the world of which the Holocaust must be the ultimate expression. But that said, he had come to the reluctant conclusion that it is indeed possible, actually necessary, to appreciate a person's intellectual contribution to the world even if that person is morally flawed. He can still appreciate the works of a flawed genius while maintaining an awareness of what they were like as human beings. On the other hand, some great historical figures were also admirable people, so he guessed all the different aspects that a person displays are independent variables.

He spent the rest of the month reading just about everything about philosophy that he could get his hands on. This included both the original works, sometimes in translation, of the great philosophers as well as various commentaries and explanations of what these profound thinkers were actually saying, or trying to say. He often found these explanations and interpretations more understandable than the original tracts. He was struck both by how verbally dense and also focussed many of the latter were, some of which seemed as sharply written as a laser beam, always exploring the consequences of the underlying thesis with meticulous energy. He tried hard to extract any relevance of these works to his own unfortunate position but that was not an easy thing to do. After all, these thinkers seemed more concerned with identifying universal truths than providing reading matter for self-help groups. He read voraciously and at great speed, something he had learned to do during his many years studying briefs as a barrister and then detailed cases as a Judge. He approached the subject logically though, re-reading many works while studying new ones from the past and steadily working forwards chronologically. He read some of the works of Plato, which impressed him with their deceptively straightforward Socratic method which was reminiscent of many a courtroom cross-examination, a little of the medieval thinkers, David Hume's convincing refutation of deductive reasoning and causality, some of the works of Spinoza, Leibnitz and Berkeley, was impressed with the utilitarianism of Mill and Bentham, struggled with the analytical logic of Bertrand Russell, and enjoyed and largely agreed with the logical positivists like Ayer. After three weeks of this intensive study he felt rather like the great physicist Enrico Fermi who, after listening to a distinguished lecturer, apparently said that before the lecture he was confused, and after the lecture he was still confused, but on a higher level. That summarised pretty well what he felt. His mind had certainly been given a good workout, that was for sure. He had certainly thought and learned a good deal, but had he truly gained any insights that could be usefully employed nearer to home? The answer to that question was yes and no. One might have predicted that response.

One thing that struck Richard was just how clever people could be throughout the ages. We have a rather arrogant tendency to favour the modern generation in matters of both knowledge and intellect, largely, he suspected, because of our vastly superior level of science and sophistication, but the hard evidence is against that. He was thinking particularly of the medieval thinkers such as St Anselm. His ontological argument for the existence of God sounds like a bit of a con, but actually no-one, not even the cleverest of philosophers, has ever been able to refute him convincingly. If one reduces his argument of inferring God's 'existence' from his 'essence', to put it quite technically, then the syllogistic argument goes like this: God, by definition, is perfect, and existence is a perfection, so therefore since God is perfect and existence is a perfection, it follows that God possesses existence. Therefore, God exists. He knows that sounds rather simplistic and absurd, but he would challenge you to disprove it convincingly. His problem with this though is more personal than intellectual. He was unable to view existence as perfect because he had seen too much suffering in others, as well as himself, to genuinely believe that though he knows that life is meant to be a gift.

While life for some lucky ones is generally wonderful, the sad reality is that for others more often than not it is tantamount to hell on earth. He supposed that if you believe in the existence of God and the afterlife (which he does not, though not for want of trying) then everything St Anselm said in the late eleventh century might be true.

He saw other evidence of the brilliance of our ancestors just after the middle ages too. Just consider the following quartet, all of whose lives encroached into the seventeenth century: Francis Bacon; the father of the modern scientific method, Isaac Newton; the scientific genius whose seminal discoveries heralded the scientific revolution and Enlightenment, Thomas Willis; the father of Neurology and brain anatomy, and William Harvey;

the discoverer of the circulation of the blood. There is no doubt about it – England has produced an abundance of intellectual giants, and he could think of numerous other examples. But herein lies the big question as he saw it. Are such geniuses, great and important as they are, true representatives of the human race or are they just exceedingly rare examples of what humans are capable of? How often might we expect an Albert Einstein to be born? Possibly just one appears every century at most. Individuals like these appear so very rarely on our landscape so we can look at such phenomena in two different ways. Either we can say mankind is truly great because every now and then giants like these appear and produce the quantum leap in our knowledge of the world that allows us to make great progress. In that sense, they are both exceedingly rare and necessary and so we should be proud to call ourselves human beings. Or else, on the other hand, we might say they are so rare that they have little to do with the vast majority of people, and that includes all the very clever ones too, as these geniuses are on a different scale of intellectual achievement. If the first of these is true, then we can rejoice that we are fellow members of a species that is capable of producing such extraordinary people. But if the second view is true then he could see very little hope or justification for the continued existence of people like him. But again, you need to be the judge of that. The month of August thus ended on a very uncertain note, and that was not what Richard was hoping for.

CHAPTER 10

September - The realm of literary possibilities

Life can become dangerous when it starts to emulate fiction. Some writers delude themselves that what they relate on paper from their imagination is a true reflection of life's realities, both good and bad, kind and cruel, real and imagined, idealised and aspirational. But if they truly believe that, then they are surely mistaken. Everyone's life is a secret, known in its entirety only to them (and occasionally not even to them), and no-one can ever encapsulate another person's inner soul whatever they may think and however many documents and apparently hard evidence they think they have uncovered. While some clever and meticulous biographers and novelists can certainly get pretty near the truth about a person's real nature, both real and self-proclaimed, there will, inevitably, always be an impenetrable barrier between the pen and the reality. If this is all true, which Richard fervently believes it is, then a person will inevitably fall into an abyss of unreality and lies if any attempt is made to live up to the fantasies written about them. His advice is never to believe the portrayed myth of one's own existence. No-one gets away for free in life and few others know just how much one suffers.

With these uncomfortable thoughts infiltrating his already troubled mind, he started that month to evaluate his own career in the Law as honestly and objectively as he possibly could, with the obvious proviso that by definition any judgement he ever made must always have been a subjective one albeit tempered with a modicum of wisdom. But that is acceptable if the judgement is also an honest one, or at least as honest as is humanly possible, which of course is an intrinsically flawed process anyway. What a circular argument we weave.

Overall, he had not done too badly to say the least, though, if he is candid, he feels he had the intrinsic ability to do better, though that never truly worried him. But in all walks of life there are missed opportunities; the real difficulty there is in knowing instinctively which of these will have had truly negative consequences. But the problem with instinct is that it is sometimes completely wrong, and no-one is naturally endowed with the gift of prophecy. The more he thinks about it then the more he realised that ruminating over what might have been is both pointless and meaningless. A different pathway, for example, may have led to a premature death within a few days and then where would we all be? No-where.

Anyway, after obtaining his Law degree he became a junior and then a senior and highly successful barrister, even if he says so himself. His secret was always to be meticulously prepared and know his brief backwards, and then to anticipate any counter-arguments in Court. He also learned the trick of thinking quickly on his feet. Initially, he was involved primarily in defending cases, but as he became more senior, he focussed much more on prosecution, especially where he could, on serious crimes. He gained a reputation for precision and thoroughness and, much to his surprise, became a QC in his mid-forties – some twenty years previously – and earned a very good living by any standards. His elderly parents, neither of whom were professional people, were very proud of him. He became part of a leading legal chambers in central London and acted in a few high-profile cases. After over fifteen years of working as a barrister he was appointed as a Circuit Court Judge and that is what he was when he retired a year previously. He generally enjoyed the work and was involved primarily in judging criminal cases which is where his main legal expertise lay. He always wore a violet robe with a lilac sash, which is the reason why some people referred to Circuit Judges as 'purple judges' which for some reason used to irritate him slightly. Well at least no-one ever called him a 'circus judge' as John Mortimer's fictional Horace Rumpole of the Bailey would have said (that is, of course, as far as he knows). When, as was usually the case, he heard criminal cases he was more formally attired, with the convention insisting that he also wore a wig and bands commensurate with the serious business of the Court. On a few occasions when he was very senior, just for the last few years of his career you understand, he was paid the honour of sitting on the Court of Appeal for criminal cases, but he never, of course, ascended to the highest ranks of his profession which as you know is to be a High Court Judge. While such an appointment would have been desirable, the truth is that he was happy enough and very busy in his daily job, so he never really hankered after or aspired to this highest legal level, even though it carried with it an automatic Knighthood or Damehood. So what, he said to himself. He had, after all, already received a gong of national recognition, so this was not an issue for him.

Novels and histories based on the legal profession have often had a distinct ring of authenticity, and he thinks this is partly because transcripts of real trials are freely available. Writers have been able to refer to what actually transpired in criminal cases, and the adversarial system of cross-examination, as well as objections and sentencing, have often been readily formulated into imagined court cases dreamed up by a succession of novelists. It seems there is a public appetite for courtroom dramas rather in the same way that people are naturally attracted to hospital soap operas and all the shenanigans they involve. While naturally he fully understands the popularity of this obsession, he has never welcomed it.

Whether he was seeking pure enjoyment or true

inspiration from reading or re-reading as many novels as he possibly could during the month of September is unclear, but he felt the most important reason was somehow to find something in a novel that had the capacity to change his mind-set and radically alter his gloomy mood after he had resigned from his profession. But he had no idea in advance whether this exercise would be successful. Though he is a fast reader, the maximum number of novels he could reasonably read in one month was about twelve, a recurring, if not ironic, number in this whole sad business. But there was surprisingly little relation between his younger literary tastes and those as a late-middle-aged adult. He remembered as a teenager being literally frightened of the nineteenth century yet finding the age of the Tudors quite attractive. He now sees that view as absurd.

He could not even bear to read anything by Charles Dickens, arguably Britain's greatest novelist, as a young man because he found the entire Victorian age so dark and intimidating. But now the opposite is true. He found great spiritual comfort from re-reading his Great Expectations and David Copperfield, yet he is now extremely wary of even imagining himself trying to survive disease or the Draconian laws and poisonous politics of the early sixteenth century. How times change. What he was trying to do was derive some form of spiritual comfort from the experience of being immersed in the daily life of another age, even if it lacked many modern advantages and luxuries. He was not referring to misplaced nostalgia for another age, an all too common pitfall for the unthinking, but to the more exciting notion of finding a common ground and sense of unity from a period of our past history. But he was not completely naive in this regard; he might find the notion of being a late-eighteenth-century English nobleman or an innovative and well-respected nineteenth-century physician-natural philosopher agreeable in principle, but the thought of no antibiotics, anaesthesia or vaccinations was still terrifying.

Notwithstanding his fear of illness in past times, he derived great stimulation and, again, actual comfort, from high-level historical novels, with the greatest affirmation of life provided by the Aubrey-Maturin seafaring novels of Patrick O'Brian. There seems to be a relatively small coterie of O'Brian devotees, of whom he was definitely one, who all derive great pleasure (and in his case, comfort too) from his original and realistic mixture of nautical history, war, friendship, food, philosophy, natural history, politics and geography. If any novel, or series of novels, can raise downcast spirits then these can certainly do the job, but during that month he only had time to re-read the first two novels in his twenty-part chronological sequence. Exactly why this kind of historical fiction, based firmly on real events, had such a positive effect he just did not know, but there are many others who have experienced something very similar. He can suggest all kinds of possible explanations for this phenomenon, but sometimes it is best to just say nothing and say a big 'Thank you' to the author whose powerful imagination and meticulous scholarship caused so much pleasure. He supposed that was the same quality that he was seeking in the works of other novelists, and in some, but not all, cases he was able to perceive this quality, this inspiration, this comfort. But, again, *chacun à son goût* as the French would say, no doubt. Thus reassured, he ended September on a largely positive note. But his intensely introspective survey also raised a possibility, or more accurately a horror, that frightened him more than anything else. What if he was slowly becoming the unwitting subject of his own novel? Perish the thought.

CHAPTER 11

October - A good time to be unselfish

Everyone should show compassion for the less fortunate at some time of their lives. Richard has always tried to show this during his legal career, though it is particularly difficult to practice what he preaches when it comes to hardened criminals and the comparatively rare examples of people who are just inherently bad. He has no problem with judging such monsters harshly. Sadly, there are a few of those truly evil individuals lurking in the edges of our landscape, but they were not his concern during the month of October. He also must admit that he has a bee in his bonnet about vitriol poisoning where corrosive acids are thrown into the victims' face producing horrific pain and scarring. He is so glad the sentencing tariff for this offence has recently been increased from a maximum of ten to twenty years imprisonment. If he had his way it would be even longer for this heinous crime which can never be justified under any circumstances. He may have a reputation as a deeply compassionate Judge, but he can also be extremely tough on occasion.

There comes a time in life when it is good to be unselfish and start helping others rather than ruminating endlessly about our own sense of failure and misfortune. Of course, one may well be a failure but that is not a sufficient reason for a failure to act. That's a subtle distinction that he needs to think about more often than he does. He is glad that he had a reputation among his peers and other colleagues as a fair and thoughtful Judge. In retrospect, he may even have been a little too lenient in his judgements and sentencing but he always believed in the somewhat hackneyed concept of personal redemption and also in giving people a second chance in life. After all, we all make big mistakes, some involuntarily, in our life, and he is convinced there are no exceptions to that notion. But for the grace of God go I, and all that stuff. Yet he only ever had two of his judgements successfully challenged in the Appeal Court. In one case he was accused of being too lenient to an outrageous insurance fraudster and the tariff was increased on appeal from his original two years in prison to three. In the other case it was considered that, though he had made an error in an interpretation of a particular law, this should have no effect on the length of the suspended sentence of one year which was allowed to stand as it was. While he disagreed with both Appeal Court judgements, naturally he accepted them with good grace, and it could have been far worse.Nevertheless, he does take considerable comfort from knowing for certain that solicitors and barristers always used to breathe a sigh of relief, tempered with many rays of hope, whenever they learned that their client was to be tried by him, His Honour Richard McQuade QC. That must be a good thing, surely.

He often wondered why we punish people at all. That might seem a bit perverse coming from a senior Judge, but the question is still a valid one. If you read what the legal philosophers and ethicists say, there are three main justification for punishing people. One is retribution for the offender's crime, another is to deter others from offending in a similar way, and the third is in order to rehabilitate the criminal. He would add a fourth reason which is to keep truly dangerous criminals far away from the public to protect them from violence. Surprisingly, you might well think, he has generally found the retribution argument to be the most justifiable, largely because it makes it possible to match the severity of the punishment to the gravity of the crime, and once the penalty is paid then, in theory, the debt to society is paid off. Yet we all know how great is the continuing stigma that ex-convicts suffer in our so-called civilised society. The deterrence argument has some justification in that it is consistent with broadly Utilitarian values, but it always has the inherent danger of punishing the innocent in the name of a higher cause. As far as rehabilitation is concerned, in his view it has one great disadvantage: from his long experience, it hardly ever works as evidenced by the almost impossible problem of serial re-offenders. My goodness, he thinks, he is sounding rather like a Judge, and that is truly not his intention here. You have his most sincere apologies.

He once heard of an extremely eminent Cardiothoracic surgeon in a leading London teaching hospital who, soon after retiring at the then mandatory age of sixty-five years (which always makes our American medical colleagues incredulous), decided to spend the rest of his life doing purely charitable work rather than continuing to earn zillions of pounds from his private medical practice. Richard knew this man had all the advantages in life such as well-to-do professional parents, a top private school education, an Oxford degree in medicine, the best junior surgical positions in London, the been-to-America (BTA) qualification, and then a top surgical consultancy at the early age of thirty-four years with a large and lucrative private practice based in London's fashionable Harley Street. You know the type of man – a suave and smooth operator in every sense of the word, with a clipped accent and wearing a spotless three-piece black pin stripe suit. But ten years after retiring, he is still spending half of every week driving a van all around the city, including the less salubrious parts, in order to ferry the infirm and the very old from their homes to day centres and various other locations. He gives no reasons for doing what he now does. He just does it, and for no reward or recognition, just the gratitude of the less fortunate. He likes that story and he suspects he is happier now than he was as a much sought-after London surgical big shot.

The question he had to ask himself was where to

begin, and, knowing that this activity would only last for one month, he had to select his sphere of benign activity with much thought and care. He lived (and still does for as long as he is lucky enough to be alive) in North London and knew that there was what was called an 'old people's home' nearby, only about two miles from where he lived. There may be better euphemisms for such an institution, but he knew it was the obvious place to make first contact. After he had made just one phone call to the chosen home offering his services, free of charge naturally, he was rather surprised at just how positive the man in charge was. His name was Don Stevenson.

'Splendid, absolutely splendid,' was his initial response.

This took him by surprise, but this may just have been a reflection of his anxiety. 'When can you start?'

'Tomorrow.'

'Good. That's splendid. Can you drive a van?'

'Yes, no problem,' he replied, truthfully, he might add (he was a particularly good and versatile driver).

'Right. Splendid. I look forward to seeing you in my office tomorrow morning. What time would best for you?' he asked.

'How about nine in the morning? That's fine for me.'

'Splendid.'

So, Richard became a van driver serving the elderly for the first week of his secondment to The Nettles Retirement Home as it was called. He was not quite sure how that title came about but he rather liked it. It comprised of two large Victorian mansions, connected by a low narrow covered passageway, and it could accommodate up to twenty-four residents. It was a private home, so it was well furnished and supplied, and he immediately noticed a distinctly happy atmosphere at every level. There was also a very healthy staff-to-resident ratio which worked well and did not surprise him. He also rather liked being an assistant chauffeur for the Home, carting elderly folk, some of whom were extremely old (by which he meant over eighty-five years) to and from various activity and entertainment venues and the Home. Don, as he was known to everyone, seemed very pleased with both his driving and the obvious personal rapport with the 'guests', as the residents were called by all the staff. As you might have guessed, he told him that his driving work was splendid.

Two weeks, and at least fifty 'splendids' later, Don and Richard agreed that he should spend the second half of the month working within the Home itself which in practice meant spending most of the time talking with the residents and helping the domestic staff hand out the lunches and mid-morning and mid-afternoon snacks. Whether it was due to the freedom from the heavy stresses of his previous job, or whether it was due to some other more positive factor, the truth is that he really enjoyed this work which gave him a high level of personal satisfaction and fulfilment that he had hardly thought possible. In short, it was a revelation, and, even better, he did not have to sift through reams of densely written papers in the evenings after work. For a brief period, he even began to think it possible that he would have been happier and generally better off if he had quit his prestigious post several years earlier than he did. That was a nice thought, but had he done so then he would never have been able to help his three children with their exorbitant flat deposits. In other words, charity really does begin at home.

During that second fortnight he managed to have several 'one to one' discussions with some of the residents, some of whom had remarkable stories to tell. He was particularly pleased to witness the great respect that almost all the staff showed to their elderly residents and not once did he witness the abhorrent, but regrettably quite common, habit of young people addressing distinguished war heroes and ex-majors, colonels and generals by their first names as if they no longer commanded any respect from their fellow humans. That type of ignorance always riles him, but in this place it did not exist. Here they were far more enlightened than in many other Institutions. A distinguished and decorated Major in the British Army is still called Major in his book. Things tend to be rather different in other cultures. In Japan, for example, the elderly are greatly respected, especially for their longevity and perceived wisdom, though in his experience this latter is not a quality that is an inevitable consequence of old age, though by dint of living a long time he supposes it should be. He was genuinely riveted by some of the stories of the Second World War that two of the old soldiers related to him in exceptional detail. There was no evidence of the slightest erosion or blurring of memory for the extraordinary events that these splendid men had witnessed and had once been part of. There was even a man who had been in the second wave on Sword beach in the D Day landings. Goodness, he had a quite a tale to tell. He asked him about the nature of bravery and whether he thought it was innate or acquired or both. He thinks the answer must have been a bit of both because, so he told him, a few soldiers did all the tough fighting, a few did virtually nothing at all but just watched events fearfully, and the majority of men could go either way depending on the quality of leadership. These latter soldiers could be as brave as lions if led well and were sufficiently motivated. He also learned, as if he did not really know this already from his own experience, that being bold and brave are two entirely different things. A very small number of soldiers are bold and experience little fear, but just perhaps anticipation. Yet the vast majority are terrified before a battle, and the truly brave ones are those who were most scared but somehow, through some internal strength, are able to conquer their fear and fight the enemy with little concern for their own safety. How he admired these people, and the stories they told, and how lucky and protected he thought his own life had been. The month of October had been a revelation and he began to be increasingly convinced that his underlying problem was finally going to be resolved in a positive way.

CHAPTER 12

November - The reality behind the screen

Richard never fully understands why almost everyone is so starstruck when they talk about movie stars or when they have the comparatively rare experience of meeting one of them in person. Even the most sophisticated and distinguished people seem to fall under this dubious spell when unwarranted admiration and irrational emotions invariably find their expression and all reason seems to fly away in the face of high celebrity. Perhaps it is just a natural part of human nature to feel humbled and honoured when confronted with personalities and actors who have come to be widely, sometimes universally, recognised through television and films. He had on occasion been similarly affected by famous people but only those who have achieved high distinction, if not legendary status, in the fields of law, medicine and science. He had never been impressed by the notion of celebrity *per se*. Some people almost seem to be famous for being famous and he had never had any time for such superficial nonsense. He was old fashioned enough to believe that one needs to earn the high esteem of others through hard work, talent, courage and genuine achievement.

Be that as it may, such irrational hero worship has almost certainly been with us since time immemorial. The social context may change, but people do not. But surely there is no harm in this so why should we be concerned in the least about what is essentially just a bit of amusing entertainment? The eighteenth and nineteenth centuries, after all, were suffused with national heroes and celebrities. That sensible view is largely true, and he was not that bothered about it except when the embracing of so-called celebrity permeates the highest levels of our intellectual institutions in the hope that it will attract both media coverage and greater funding. So money rears its ugly head yet again. He thinks it was ever thus in one way or another.

From time to time he had encountered high-profile clients in legal cases brought before him, and the key imperative is to treat them with the utmost fairness and as if they are just another case on which one needs to make a considered judgement. One must not be influenced in the least by their national or international fame. His medical friends and colleagues will say exactly the same thing and have told him that in their experience it is the more senior doctors and staff who are the most impressed by having famous patients in their hospital wards, far more so than the younger members of staff and the nurses looking after them. That did surprise him a little. They tell him that less treatment is tantamount to no treatment at all so a professional approach is vital. The same pertains in Court but in the final analysis we are all of us only human. He thinks a key problem is the conflation of the actor and the role he or she has played on the screen and the naive but very understandable tendency we all have to assume, probably unconsciously, that the person we see before us is the same person we have seen on the television or movie screen. He knows it's all rather absurd but that is the modern world we all inhabit.

That said, he does greatly enjoy watching movies, either in the cinema, both specialised and multiplex, and the home in the form of a DVD. So, he decided to spend the month of November indulging himself in every film of interest that he could get his hands on in the rather forlorn hope that he might derive some sense of satisfaction or inspiration that would help him make a final decision about his life. Frankly, while this was always likely to be an enjoyable set of experiences, it was never going to solve any personal problems. That is obvious to anyone with any common sense. There is obviously only a limited number of films that it is possible to watch in a relatively short time so, again, it was important to be selective in his choices. He wanted to represent different emotions and aspects of the human character, and to that end decided to evoke such things as laughter, a sense of duty, spirituality, horror, history and the world of imagination. While that was the noble intention, what eventually transpired represented a very mixed bag and ended up as largely a consequence of his innate preferences, ones that had been set many years ago.

When he was a teenager watching 'Duck Soup', one of the best and funniest films in the canon of the Marx Brothers comedies, he remembers laughing so much that he had difficulty breathing. Eventually he recovered, but their magic, though now a little dated, still amuses him greatly though not quite so forcefully, perhaps because the element of surprise no longer exists. He doesn't know whether laughter is good for one's health, but this is a medicine that does not know how to fail. Mel Brooks' humour also has the ability to render him almost senseless with laughter in its own idiosyncratic way, but he doubts such films could now be made in the current climate of extreme political correctness. His personal view on this, with which you may or may not agree, is that if we all respected each other more, and practised unfailing courtesy in our lives, then there would no longer be a need for this unfortunate reality of modern living.

The greatest spiritual shock he ever experienced from a film when he was evolving from an adolescent to a young man was delivered by 'A Man for All Seasons', with Paul Scofield in the main role of Sir Thomas More. When he decided to see this again just a few months ago he could fully understand why he was so strongly affected. More's nobility of spirit and deep love of learning had literally changed him overnight from a rather idle schoolboy more intent on doing well in the Boy Scouts and reading Marvel comics to a studious youth who studied the classics and modern literature with a degree of enthusiasm that was a source of amazement to his teachers (or 'masters' as he was obliged to call these earnest men). But of course, while his behavioural transformation was real enough, the reason for it was probably a bit of a sham. In reality, Thomas More, though clearly possessed of a fine and penetrating intellect and firmly held and honest principles, was more of a religious extremist who believed in the primacy of Papal authority and by all accounts dealt severely with those whom he regarded as heretics. Richard greatly admired his Utopia, but he no longer hero worshipped the man who wrote it, great as he undoubtedly was. The man portrayed in the remarkable film, still one of his favourites, was a very different one than in real life in the Tudor age, one that he now finds distinctly frightening. Interestingly, there is a fine and justly famous portrait by Holbein of Thomas More hanging in Lincoln's Inn, one of the four Inns of Court in London which of course he knows extremely well. In it he looks youthful and vibrant but also just a little severe. But Richard will still be eternally grateful to the man, both real and imagined.

He also spent a week sitting through a whole series of war films, a genre which he has always enjoyed and admired though he knows in his heart that this probably reflects a failing in his character rather than a shared sense of nationalistic pride. Not that he liked the sight of violence or blood– far from it; he hates watching that sort of thing even if fabricated in movies. He supposes his fondness for such films springs more from a sense of admiration and imagined nostalgia for an age that he had never experienced more than anything else. But it's still a bit of a mystery.

But he saved the best to the end of the month. He had viewed the Powell and Pressburger masterpiece 'A Matter of Life and Death' many times during his life spanning youth to middle age, and if any film had relevance to his current mental predicament then it was assuredly this one. The sheer cleverness of the storyline, the enigmatic nature of the main characters, the subtlety of the illness portrayed, the innovative and dreamlike sets, and the final life-enhancing denouement erased his doubts about life while raising spirituality to an art form.

CHAPTER 13

December: The cycle of life and death

In December he decided to contemplate the nature of the Universe. He knows he is ambitious, but he did say contemplate and not understand. No-one on earth is capable of doing that. Maybe no-one ever will. But that limitation does not detract from the mental ingenuity of our human species in building complex models of our galaxy and beyond, and the mind-boggling precision of their calculations and practical astronomical measurements. There are for sure a lot of very clever people out there.

During that first week of the month Richard spent every evening from about nine until midnight endlessly viewing the night sky from his large rectangular garden, a space which had previously been a floral showpiece, but which had now become his own private zone of observation, known only to himself. Its function had been transformed into a learning space as each day merged seamlessly into evening and night. He had been a keen amateur astronomer in his twenties, just forty years previously, and had retained a few but important elements of basic knowledge of the heavens. As a boy he used to have a four-inch reflecting telescope but by then as an adult all that he possessed was a fine pair of powerful army-grade binoculars. Besides, he was an avid follower of popular science and had always maintained a keen awareness of man's likely place in the Universe. Reassuringly, he could still recognise many of the better-known constellations which were easily visible in the vast sky when the night was clear from dusty and luminal contamination and the cloud covering was light. He knew that we humans had about one hundred billion nerve cells, or neurons, within our brains and this was also the same as the estimated number of galaxies in our known Universe. When he then remembered that our own Galaxy contains about three hundred billion stars, he realised there must be an almost unimaginably large number of stars in our Galaxy, not to mention the Universe. Yet there are presumably many other Universes as well as our own.

Surely, at least a few of the zillions of stars out there must have planets whizzing around them that can support some kind of life? And what about their laws? He does not mean the natural physical laws that we have discovered over the centuries and are, he presumes, the same everywhere in our Universe (but perhaps not in other Universes, assuming these exist). No, he means the laws that govern peoples' behaviour, the rule of law that he has always tried to uphold. Surely, they must be different in other Worlds? After all, laws are different even within the United Kingdom if you compare certain English laws with Scottish laws, not to mention the much greater differences between Western legal systems and those in the Gulf states. No-one knows for sure whether that is even a meaningful question. The problem is, you will understand, that he just could not imagine or indeed accept that we are totally alone in the Universe. He will never know for certain which is one of the very few things that he does actually know for certain. If we really are alone then we are very special, and if we are not alone then we are still existing in a very special Galaxy. Either way, he reasoned, not totally irrationally, there was a total justification for celebration and living one's life to the full.

So, Richard started serious stargazing in those late evenings when it was both cold and dark as the annual misery of winter had already settled in with its customary ruthlessness. But the more he gazed towards the stars then the more he started to feel part of the Universe, and he was gradually moving inexorably nearer to a final decision to choose life rather than death. As if instructed or controlled by some kind of higher force or entity, he began to feel as if he was emerging from a strange darkness, one that had surreptitiously permeated his being and almost overwhelmed him with its insidious power. It was a genuine enlightenment in more than one sense of the word. So, after one year of deep reflection he concluded that there is life before death and that he would definitely choose to live on as long as he possibly could. He had posed a supremely dark question, reflected on it in great detail for a year, and then finally reached a logical conclusion. That was indeed a job well done.

Then the world changed, not in aeons, but over the course of a few short days.

The whole thing came on slowly but attacked him

quickly. Just after the end of the first week of December, by which time he had definitely decided not to take his own life but to live on happily until his nineties and perhaps beyond, he began to experience back pain. It was a gnawing, aching rather than a sharp pain, and, at first, he paid little attention to it and dismissed it as probably a touch of indigestion. But the pain persisted and became particularly bad at night, preventing him from sleeping well. The pain was in the middle of his back and was definitely relieved somewhat by leaning forwards. He was not a doctor, but he gathered later that this is a significant feature. He had also noticed a small loss of his usually healthy appetite, slight nausea, and had experienced an effortless half-stone weight loss over the previous three weeks which he had ignored at first because he always had to watch his weight, especially with all the lawyers' dinners he constantly gets invited to, and he was rather pleased to see the weighing scales showing a downward trend. It is amazing how we have this undoubted tendency to ignore worrying physical symptoms. It is officially called 'denial.'

It was his highly perceptive wife Joan who strongly encouraged him to see his family doctor, the avuncular General Practitioner who was in reality young enough to be his son. He was given a comparatively rare urgent appointment and he spent a full twenty minutes talking to and then examining him. While inscrutable throughout, he could perceive the very real concern in his demeanour which slowly changed from one of light joviality to obvious worry. At that point Richard also became worried, and for the first time, especially when he referred him urgently to a well-respected and highly experienced senior consultant physician at the leading teaching hospital not that far from his home.

The initial consultation with the hospital specialist, who he found out from a quick computer search had published extensively on gastro-intestinal malignancies, was quicker and more business-like than he had anticipated. Though perfectly friendly, he was also inscrutable and totally professional, and arranged for him to have a large number of urgent investigations, including numerous blood tests, a CT (Computerised Tomography) scan of his abdomen, chest and pelvis and a bone scan. All these were carried out within one week, indicating a degree of urgency that only reinforced his growing concern that he could well be in very serious medical trouble.

He was not wrong to be so concerned. The following represents a brief snapshot of the consultation with the specialist which took place just one week after completion of the investigations. It took place in the small but scrupulously clean outpatient room in the recently refurbished wing of the hospital. It is as accurate as his recent memory of those events will allow:

Specialist: Ah, Mr McQuade, good to see you. How have you been since I last saw you?

RMcQ: I've been about the same, but I have lost some more weight… rather worrying.

Specialist: Right. How about the back pain? Are the tablets I gave you helping?

RMcQ: They help slightly, and they have made a bit of a difference though I've had to increase the number I have been taking.

Specialist: Yes of course…

RMcQ: So, do you have all my test results?

Specialist: Yes, everything is now back. Let me take you through the results.

RMcQ: Yes, please do. I have a bad feeling about this I have to admit.

There was a five second pause at that point when the specialist moved rhythmically from left to right in his chair, in obvious discomfort.

Specialist: Well I am afraid your instincts were right…

RMcQ: (smiling slightly, ironically) Ah I see. Tell me the worst please.

Specialist: Well it's like this… I'm afraid the CT scan clearly shows that you have advanced pancreatic cancer.

RMcQ: Right. I thought as much to be honest. I suspected I had cancer.

Specialist: Yes. Let me show you the scans.

At this point he displayed the CT images onto a computer screen and showed Richard the large shadow in what he identified as the pancreas. The whole thing looked pretty meaningless to him. It could just as well have been the far side of the moon.

Specialist: Richard, you can see the tumour in the pancreas clearly there…

RMcQ: Yes, I see that but why do you say the cancer is advanced?

Specialist: Good question… because we have also identified secondary tumour deposits in the lymph nodes nearby as well as the lung and liver. And there is also a suspicious area in one of your long bones, though not your spine. Do you have any bone pain at all?

RMcQ: (increasingly subdued) No, I haven't.

Specialist: Would you like me to show you these other areas?

RMcQ: No thanks I'll take your word for it. How bad exactly is this particular cancer?

Specialist: To be truthful…

RMcQ: Yes, the truth, and the whole truth, would be much appreciated. I can take it.

Specialist: I'm afraid this is one of the worst cancers to have in terms of response to treatment and prognosis - the outlook that is.

RMcQ: So how long do you think it will take to kill me? How long have I got?

Specialist: Well as you know everyone is different and some people can live for many years but in general the outlook is not all good…

RMcQ: How bad do you reckon in my case? You told me it's advanced.

Specialist: On average people in your situation would be expected to survive for about four months, though that time could be doubled with treatment. Overall, about one in five people with this particular cancer survive for one year after the initial diagnosis has been made.

RMcQ: Good God, that is a pretty short time.

Specialist: Yes, I'm afraid it is. That's the problem with this particular cancer. You see it tends to present late after secondary spread to nearby organs has already occurred.

RMcQ: So, it becomes too late to treat it effectively.

Specialist: Exactly. That's the key problem.

RMcQ: So, what is the treatment?

Specialist: In the early stage, before it has spread, the tumour can be removed surgically. Surgery can also be used at a later stage to bypass any severe blockage and alleviate some of the symptoms.

RMcQ: But you wouldn't do that in my case?

Specialist: No, we wouldn't. But we could try a course of chemotherapy to try to at least slow down the course of disease. It wouldn't cure it, but it might prolong your survival a bit.

RMcQ: Chemotherapy has some nasty side-effects though. Isn't that right?

Specialist: Yes, it has.

RMcQ: Can you tell me what might happen with chemotherapy?

Specialist: Well everyone reacts differently to

chemotherapy, which we would give you via a vein and in the hospital of course. I would need to discuss all this with my oncologist colleague, but it would probably be one or two full courses. The potential side-effects include such things as hair loss, nausea and vomiting, bowel disturbance, tiredness and anaemia, and suppression of the normal immune system making you more susceptible to infections.

RMcQ: That's quite a list.

Specialist: It is, you're right, but you wouldn't be likely to get all these side-effects and some people tolerate it pretty well.

RMcQ: Well I will need to think about that. I may want to just live what remains of my life without ruining its quality. I mean… is there really any point in trying any treatment at all given the awful outlook?

Specialist: Well that's certainly one option which I would completely understand if you decide to go down that road.

RMcQ: I think 'going down' is the operative word there! I think I will need to discuss this with my wife and think about it.

Specialist: Yes, I agree that would be the best thing to do at this stage.

RMcQ: A good choice of words there – 'stage' – don't you think?

Specialist: (slightly embarrassed) Ah yes, I see what you mean. No pun intended.

RMcQ: And no offence taken.

Specialist: Right.

RMcQ: How much pain will there be… I mean later on… near the end?

Specialist: That's difficult to predict, but one thing I can tell you for sure is that whatever pain you do get will be completely controllable with modern painkillers. You will inevitably worry about that, but you needn't.

RMcQ: Can you guarantee that?

Specialist: Yes, one hundred percent.

RMcQ: Well it's good to have certainty on at least something.

Specialist: Indeed.

RMcQ: One last question for you. Why do you think I got this disease? Was I at high risk?

Specialist: Richard, I can't explain why you got pancreatic cancer. We just don't understand it well enough. We do know that certain factors can put someone at a higher risk, things such as smoking, which, by the way, is the most important, obesity, diabetes, and chronic pancreatitis, but you have none of these risk factors and were perfectly healthy. My guess is that it was all due to just a random mutation in your genetic code that in some way led to this disease.

RMcQ: Ah, genetics again.

Specialist: Yes… probably.

Well, that is what happened in the second half of December last year. The consultant was certainly straight with him and the cancer was an aggressive one and within a short time Richard was riddled with it. But the specialist was also as good as his word since his back pain, which got much worse, was completely controlled with analgesics. That inevitably included opioid medications like morphine but that was a completely necessary evil. It was ironic but he needed them. His wife and colleagues thought he was very brave in the way he reacted to this terrible blow that life had delivered to him but, perhaps because of his musings over the previous year, this accepting attitude came naturally to him and at no stage did he break down or panic. But he did not want to face his own death and he was more terrified than his friends and relatives could ever have guessed.

Then he saw the irony behind all that had happened over this previous year. When he was apparently healthy (and who knows for how long he had been harbouring this cancer that was soon to kill him) but deeply upset about no longer working or feeling useful, he had a choice to live well or die and he was frankly hell-bent on killing himself. He saw no other option at the time. Then, at the very end of his one-year experiment of trying to enhance his sensory and aesthetic experiences, he was on the verge of affirming life. But at that precise moment he found out he was very sick and would soon die. But now he was afraid of death whereas before when he was well (or at least thought he was well) he had no fear of death whatsoever. What kind of a crazy world is it where the fear of death only occurs when it is actually about to happen? At the very point that he realised life was definitely worth living he has this optimistic possibility taken away from him in the cruellest way possible. Well, Richard wished for death and now he has been given what he wished for. That's always a risky thing to do. For some people the fear of death instils a belief in God, but in his case that fear was quite enough to suppress any other fears or beliefs he might have. Everyone fears their extinction in their own particular way. But truly it wasn't what he really wanted. His late mother's attempt at a truism is completely right after all – 'Without your health you have nothing.'

Nothing whatsoever.

Printed in Great Britain
by Amazon